"I rather

you disliked

Tania said it as lightly as she could. James's hand was still resting on her nape.

"Dislike?" His voice had an odd note to it. "Is that what you really thought? No, it wasn't dislike that made me so aggressive. It was desire . . . desire and sheer jealousy."

James in love with her. It couldn't be true—but before she could say so, he was kissing her. The first real kiss she'd ever received, she realized shakily. As James released her mouth, he framed her face with his hands.

"Is it the same for you, then?" he whispered softly against her lips.

Which of them was trembling, or was it both of them?

"I think so," she admitted shakily. "I'm not used to this kind of thing."

PENNY JORDAN was constantly in trouble in school because of her inability to stop daydreaming—especially during French lessons. In her teens, she was an avid romance reader, although it didn't occur to her to try writing one herself until she was older. "My first half-dozen attempts ended up ingloriously," she remembers, "but I persevered, and one manuscript was finished." She plucked up the courage to send it to a publisher, convinced her book would be rejected. It wasn't, and the rest is history! Penny is married and lives in Cheshire.

Penny Jordan's striking mainstream novel *Power Play* quickly became a *New York Times* bestseller. She followed that success with *Silver*, a story of ambition, passion and intrigue and *The Hidden Years*, a novel that lays bare the choices all women face in their search for love.

Books by Penny Jordan

HARLEQUIN PRESENTS
1404—UNSPOKEN DESIRE
1418—RIVAL ATTRACTIONS
1427—OUT OF THE NIGHT
1442—GAME OF LOVE
1456—A KIND OF MADNESS
1476—SECOND TIME LOVING

Don't miss any of our special offers. Write to us at the following address for information on our newest releases.

Harlequin Reader Service
P.O. Box 1397, Buffalo, NY 14240
Canadian address: P.O. Box 603,
Fort Erie, Ont. L2A 5X3

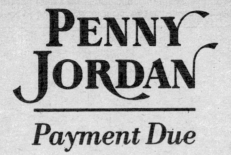

PENNY JORDAN

Payment Due

Harlequin Books

TORONTO • NEW YORK • LONDON
AMSTERDAM • PARIS • SYDNEY • HAMBURG
STOCKHOLM • ATHENS • TOKYO • MILAN
MADRID • WARSAW • BUDAPEST • AUCKLAND

Harlequin Presents first edition September 1992
ISBN 0-373-11491-5

Original hardcover edition published in 1991
by Mills & Boon Limited

PAYMENT DUE

CHAPTER ONE

THERE, that was the window display finished. Tania climbed out of the window and, opening the door, went round to the front of the shop to stand on the pavement and study her handiwork.

With the children due back at school from their summer holidays within a fortnight, it had all been rather a rush to get the shop open in time to take advantage of the potential back-to-school trade in children's shoes, but somehow or other she had managed it, developing along the way a firmness that surprised even her. But, as she had quickly discovered once she had taken the decision to start her business, there were plenty of people around who were only too eager to take advantage of her naïveté and inexperience if they could, often cloaking their callousness in the guise of appearing helpful and concerned.

She had lost track of the number of people who had warned her that her whole venture was a waste of time... that opening a shoe shop catering exclusively for children was madness, especially when she had chosen as her venue a small Cheshire market town. Everyone knew that these days people wanted to shop quickly and efficiently and that the places they chose to do so in were the huge soulless shopping malls.

Tania had listened to them, but had stubbornly stuck to her guns. She was a mother herself and she knew quite well that when it came to buying her daughter Lucy's shoes, she preferred to do so in comfort, with the help of an assistant who knew what he or she was talking about . . . someone who had been properly trained to measure a child's foot and advise on the suitability of the footwear needed.

And as for her decision to start up her business in this quiet town; well, that had been spawned by several factors, chief among which had been the fact that the property she had inherited from her unknown great-aunt, which had enabled her to make the decision in the first place had been a run-down old-fashioned draper's shop here in Appleford.

One of the most important lessons Tania had learned in life was to make the most of the opportunities fate handed to her. It would perhaps have been easier to give in to the kindly pressure of her great-aunt's bankers and to sell the shop as it stood, but she had seen in it a means of escape for Lucy and herself from the life they had been living in their small high-rise city flat with its lack of amenities, its claustrophobia, its soulless concrete lifelessness.

She had taken one look at Appleford, seen its small country town prettiness, its surrounding green fields, its open skies, its children who enjoyed the kind of environment she had always dreamed of for Lucy, and her mind had been made up.

Since the only business she had any experience of had been gained through her part-time job in a shoe shop in the city, it had seemed a natural course of events to make the decision to reopen her great-aunt Sybil's shop, but as a children's shoe shop.

She had not rushed into the decision lightly, no matter what others might think.

In the six months since she had received the astounding news that a great-aunt she had never known she had possessed had died, and that she was her sole heir, she had put herself heart and soul into making her projected new business a success.

She had been on government training courses to equip her to run the administrative side of her new business. She had learned how to deal with the various tradesmen whose services she had needed to transform the decaying, run-down shop into the pretty bow-fronted eye-catching emporium it was today. She had tackled her great-aunt's bank manager and persuaded him to advance her the money for her new venture on the strength of the building, with the shop and its upstairs flat as security. She had even taken a course in the correct fitting and selling of children's shoes, and through it all she had been praying desperately that her venture would succeed. So much depended on it.

Already Lucy was a different child from the pinched wan-faced ten-year-old whom she had feared was growing up far too fast in their potentially morally destructive inner city environment.

Perhaps it was because she herself had grown up in the country that she had felt this almost atavistic desire to return to the slower pace of country life, to a more natural and less stress-inducing atmosphere.

It was too late now to regret that she had never known her great-aunt. No doubt she had had her reasons for not making herself known to her, for allowing her to grow up believing herself to be completely alone in the world. A car accident had left her orphaned when she was twelve years old—a vulnerable age for any child—and the abrupt change in her lifestyle, from the only child of loving, caring parents to merely one of many children growing up under the harassed and over-burdened eyes of a series of foster parents, had caused her to withdraw inside herself, to become very much a loner.

Those years were now years she preferred not to remember, not to dwell on. Those years had culminated in Lucy's birth, Lucy who was so precious and dear to her, despite the fact that at first she had not wanted her.

She had discovered at eighteen that she was pregnant by a boy she barely knew; a boy who had forced himself on her, practically raping her, she had since realised with the hindsight of maturity and wisdom.

At the time she had been too afraid, had felt too guilty, had believed that she herself was too much to blame to tell anyone what had happened.

They had met at a party; a party to which she had gone unwillingly with a girl with whom she had worked. She had left the foster home by then and had been living in a cramped council flat along with three other girls in similar positions to herself.

No doubt because of the various traumas of their lives, none of them, including herself, had been the type to reach out to others, to make friends easily, to trust easily, and so she had had no one with whom to discuss the tragedy which had overwhelmed her when she had realised she was pregnant.

The boy whom she had only known as 'Tommy' was someone she never wanted to see again. The shock of his possession of her had left scars which had taken a long time to heal and by the time she had plucked up the courage to confide in her doctor it was far too late for her to have her pregnancy terminated, even if she had wanted to do so.

Then she had been desolate, anguished, frantic with fear and resentment. Emotions she had continued to experience right up until the moment the midwife had placed Lucy in her arms.

Then she had known that no matter how difficult it might be, no matter what she was forced to endure in order to do so, she must keep her daughter.

There had been privations, hardships. She had hated the necessity of accepting aid from the state, but had had no alternative.

Even so, just as soon as she could, just as soon as Lucy had been at school, she had found herself a part-time job and somehow or other she had managed to make ends meet, but the pressure of her perilous financial situation had been constant and draining. There was no relief from it, no money for even the smallest of luxuries or extras.

So many, many times she had looked at Lucy, wearing the second-hand clothes she had lovingly washed and pressed, and ached to be able to clothe her daughter in things that were hers alone, ached to give her the kind of treats Lucy saw being enjoyed by other children.

It had hurt her sometimes to see the wistful longing in Lucy's eyes and to know that it was out of love for her, out of a knowledge that no child of her age should ever have had, that she never once begged or pleaded for treats.

She had not been the only single parent living in the massive, desolate tower block of council flats. She had made friends with several of the other mothers, and she knew she would miss their down-to-earth company, now that she and Lucy were finally established in Appleford.

Before leaving she had pressed upon them fervent invitations to come and see her, anxious not to lose touch with the few people with whom she had managed to form a genuine bond.

All of them had tragic, unhappy tales to tell: some of husbands who had deserted them, leaving them with young dependent children; some who had done the leaving, driven from their homes by men who abused them physically and emotionally.

Some, like her, had found themselves mothers virtually before they were adult themselves. All of them shared a gritty, fierce determination to see that their children would not suffer as they had, to ensure that somehow their children would inherit a better, wiser, more compassionate world.

Yes, she would miss their support, their friendship, and they would not be easy to replace. She didn't make friends easily, preferring her own company. Another legacy from her past; a deep-rooted fear, perhaps, of allowing herself to get too close to anyone because she feared the eventual pain of losing them.

No, it was for Lucy's sake that she had taken this dangerous step into a new world. It was because for Lucy she wanted so much more than she had had herself. Not necessarily more in a material sense; it was going to be a long time before the business allowed them to live any more luxuriously than they had done in the city.

But at least here, with the clean, fresh air and the wide-open horizons, Lucy would have the benefit of an environment a hundred times better than the one she had had in the city.

Already she had told Tania in amazed accents that, in her new school, there would only be twenty other children in her class. In the city she had shared a classroom with almost sixty other pupils. Here the children had access to playing fields, to tennis courts, to a local sports centre, which, unlike the one in the city, was not a long bus ride away through the heart of a city in which no sensible unescorted woman walked after dark, and certainly where no mother could allow her child to venture unprotected.

Yes, she had made the right decision, no matter how many people might shake their heads and predict failure for her.

She might not be able to provide Lucy with the secure emotional background that came from two loving parents who were committed to one another and to the welfare of their children, but at least she was doing the best she could for her.

And, anyway, marriage wasn't always the blissful, self-fulfilling, self-contained state of happiness and security those on the outside of it tended to imagine.

Take Nicholas Forbes, for instance, her late relative's solicitor and now her own. He had a beautiful wife, the stepsister of a very wealthy local businessman, two healthy children, a successful practice, a home on the outskirts of the town in one of its most prestigious areas, which Tania had heard a rumour had been given to them as a wedding present by Clarissa Forbes's stepbrother, and yet, according to local gossip, Nicholas Forbes and his wife were far from happy.

And it was not only gossip. Nicholas himself had indicated as much to her before she could stop him and make it plain to him that the last thing she wanted was to involve herself in anyone else's private life. That the very last thing she appreciated in any man was what was to her an outright betrayal of the trust and privacy which should exist between a committed couple. Personally she thought it extremely disloyal for one partner in a relationship to discuss the private problems of that relationship with an outsider, especially when that outsider was not a properly trained counsellor or adviser. Besides, she barely knew Nicholas Forbes. As her solicitor, she had found his advice, his willingness to put himself out for her and help her with all the many small problems involved in setting up her small business, heart-warming and encouraging, making her think that perhaps her years of determinedly distancing herself from the entire male sex were now something she ought to outgrow. She had liked Nicholas, but not specifically as a man. She had liked him as a person, a fellow human being, but sexually... She made a tiny moue.

Sexually she was completely immune to any and all members of the male sex and that was the way she wanted things to stay.

She was an intelligent woman. She realised that not all men were necessarily like Lucy's father, that even he might have found maturity and wisdom as he grew up. But, despite her awareness that logically not all men had to be disliked and shunned, emotionally and as far as her body was concerned, physically, she only felt safe and in control when they were held at a good distance.

She did her best not to communicate her fear, her dislike to Lucy. Idealistically, maternally, she wanted for her daughter all that she had not had herself and that included the self-confidence, the freedom, the belief in herself and in others which would enable her to reach out when the time came and to forge the kind of emotional and physical bonds with another human being which she had never been able to.

For Lucy she wanted it all: happiness, success, security. She would never encourage her daughter to consider herself less of a human being because she was female. She would bring her up in a full awareness of her own assets. Most of all for Lucy she wanted the security that came from knowing that she would never ever have to depend on anyone else, either emotionally or materially.

Lucy was a clever child, a child who would do so much better in a smaller school environment where she would receive more individual tuition and attention. She also made friends easily, something which she herself had never been able to do.

She had no fears of Lucy being isolated or alone in their new home. Already she had made friends with another girl whose family lived half a dozen doors away. Her parents owned and ran a local decorating shop, her father was a decorator, and it had been he who had papered the awkward-to-deal-with ceilings in their own upstairs flat, cheerfully managing the sloping ceilings of the old eighteenth-century building.

Ann and Tom Fielding were a pleasant couple in their late thirties. Susan was their youngest child, and had two older brothers, and, although Tania had felt her normal reticence with Tom Fielding, despite his genuine kindness, she had felt very drawn to Ann Fielding's warm personality.

The couple had gone out of their way to welcome her to the local community, giving her generous advice about her potential business and making both Lucy and herself welcome in their home.

Their own shop, unlike hers, was double-fronted, with a generous-sized flat above it in which Ann Fielding had allowed her artistic talents full licence.

Tania had marvelled at the effect of her marbled bathroom, a painting technique which Ann had modestly assured her was quite easy to pick up.

In addition, their property, like her own, had a long rear garden, but, unlike her wilderness, theirs was neatly segmented into a pretty courtyard for sitting in, plus a well-maintained vegetable plot, the sight of which had made her own fingers itch to get to grips with her smaller garden.

Lucy was round at the Fieldings' now, and Tania broke off her contemplation of her shop window, with its artistically draped 'branch' and its tumble of fallen gold and russet leaves in shades that toned with the display of winter brogues and boots, to glance at her watch.

Heavens, was it really that time already? Lucy would be beginning to think she had abandoned her. The window display had taken longer than she had expected, and then there had been that long telephone call from a supplier. It was time she changed out of her scruffy working jeans and T-shirt and went round to the Fieldings.

Ann Fielding had very kindly invited both of them to join her family for tea, an invitation which Tania had hesitantly accepted, not wanting to take too much advantage of Ann Fielding's generosity and uncomfortably conscious that as yet she was not in a position to repay her hospitality.

In fact it was an invitation she would probably have refused if it weren't for the fact that last night, totally out of the blue, just as she and Lucy had been about to sit down, her solicitor, Nicholas Forbes, had arrived unannounced and unexpected, explaining that he was on his way past and had thought he would call.

Tania wasn't used to having men in her home and neither was Lucy, and Tania had been conscious of a feeling of resentment and irritation which she had tried to repress. After all, Nicholas Forbes was merely being kind, merely being friendly. And yet... And yet...

Was she wrong in imagining that there had been something in the way he had eyed her T-shirt and jeans-clad figure, something that, while not remotely lustful, had not been entirely without sexual curiosity either?

She had come a long way from the inexperienced girl of eighteen who had silently endured the painful fumblings of the much stronger and heavier boy who had been her first and only sexual partner. She knew a good deal more about the human race now at twenty-nine than she had done at eighteen. Sex was something she avoided, something she had cut out of her life. She felt no sexual desire, no sexual curiosity, and had no need of a man in her life in any sexual sense, and that was the way she preferred it.

There had been men who had attempted to change her attitude, but she had always firmly and determinedly rebuffed them, making it clear that they were wasting their time, and she had no idea why on earth a man like Nicholas Forbes with a wife as attractive as Clarissa Forbes should show any interest in a woman like her, who could not afford to dress in anything other than the cheapest chainstore clothes, who could never afford the money or the time to visit a hairdresser or beauty salon, whose hands were serviceable rather than elegant, with short unpainted nails—hands which were far more used to the hard realities of life than the sensual pleasures. Unless it was because she was on her own.

She had come up against that particular phenomenon too often and from too many unlikely sources to be naïve about it any more. The most unlikely men could betray the most unwelcome sexual harassment when it suited them. There had been that teacher of Lucy's who had called round to the flat on the pretext of wanting to discuss her work. There had been her superior at the shoe shop. There had been countless others, all of them no doubt respectable and well-thought-of men, but all of them, as far as she was concerned, men who were being disloyal to their wives and families, to whom they most owed commitment.

Personally she could think of no reason why Nicholas Forbes should want to spend time with her. She was not pretty, not in the way that his wife was. Tania had seen her once when she had called at Nicholas's office, bursting into the room and totally ignoring Tania, and she was a pretty, fluffy blonde woman in her early thirties, with a slightly petulant, spoilt expression and the mannerisms of a little girl.

Tania hadn't been particularly drawn to her. Just listening to her pouting little girl demands as she persuaded Nicholas to agree to her plans for re-decorating their drawing-room had confirmed Tania's initial view that as women they were complete opposites.

She doubted if Clarissa Forbes had ever wanted for anything in her entire life. The clothes she was wearing were expensive designer models, her hair, her hands, everything about her proclaimed that Clarissa was an adored, petted woman whose single most important preoccupation in life was herself and her own needs.

She was barely five feet two with round blue eyes and a pretty-pretty face, making Tania at five feet seven, with her thick, heavy mane of conker-brown hair and her cheap cotton skirt and blouse, feel uncomfortably conscious of the difference between them.

Perhaps because no one had ever told her so, Tania herself was unaware of the classic beauty of her oval face, with its high cheekbones and well defined lines. She had no idea that the length of her neck and the fullness of her mouth gave her a sensual vulnerability that men found fascinating, or that her lack of artifice, her inability to pretend and pout, might be like a much-needed glass of clean, pure water to a man who had come to feel sickened by the syrupy mock sweetness of a wife who could turn into a virago the moment she was opposed in any way.

Because she had no wish to attract the male sex, Tania assumed that they felt no attraction towards her. Certainly she did nothing to attract their attention or desire. Certainly she never encouraged them to believe that she wanted or needed them in any way, and, because she was the woman she was, she genuinely had no idea that her very indifference, her very lack of interest, only caused men to be more attracted to her, more curious about her, more determined to breach the walls she had so obviously put up around herself.

She had got rid of Nicholas Forbes just as quickly as she could, firmly explaining that she considered this particular time of day sacrosanct to Lucy. Undeterred, Nicholas Forbes had offered to take her out for a drink so that they could talk in private, but she had quickly refused.

She felt that she had made it more than plain to him that, while she welcomed his conscientiousness as her solicitor, there could be no personal relationship between them, especially one that involved the kind of discussions about his marriage which she knew could only lead to problems.

Even if the kind of friendship he had been offering her *had* included Clarissa, even if Clarissa herself had been willing to welcome her to their circle of friends, which she quite plainly was not, Tania doubted if she would have felt comfortable with them. The Forbeses, while not jet-setters, certainly had a very comfortable and affluent lifestyle. Ann Fielding had mentioned in conversation that Clarissa's brother was an extremely wealthy man and that through his various companies and contacts he had put a good deal of business Nicholas's way.

'I was at school with Nick,' she had added, pulling a face as she commented, 'Perhaps I shouldn't say so, but I suspect that, as far as his marriage is concerned, he's beginning to discover that marrying a rich girl isn't all a bed of roses. Clarissa is very spoilt. James dotes on her and spoils her to death. It's amazing how stupid even the most intelligent of men can be, isn't it? There's only three or four years between them; James's father was Clarissa's mother's second husband and both of them were killed in a skiing accident just before Clarissa's twentieth birthday. She went completely to pieces and although legally she was an adult, James stepped in and virtually took the place of their parents overnight, and he's gone on shielding and protecting her ever since. Too much so, if you ask me. He's made a rod for his own back in indulging her so much. She's very possessive about him, and I doubt if she's ever going to allow any woman he becomes involved with to oust her as number one in his life, which is a shame, really.'

'Perhaps he enjoys their relationship,' Tania suggested. 'Some men seem to get a kick out of keeping the women in their lives dependent on them either emotionally or financially.'

Her comment had earned her a shrewd, thoughtful look from Ann Fielding and the comment, 'Some do, yes, but I wouldn't put James Warren in that class. He's far too intelligent, too…too secure in himself emotionally to need that kind of hold on another human being. No, I think he's simply grown so used to believing that Clarissa needs him that he can't see the truth about her, and she, of course, takes good care that he doesn't see it. She isn't at all popular locally. Most people feel rather sorry for Nicholas, even though they also feel that he's rather brought his own misery down upon himself. Clarissa will never be satisfied with anything that Nicky can give her, not while she's so aware of the difference between the lifestyle she had with James and the lifestyle that Nicky can provide for her.'

'But they seem very comfortably off,' Tania hadn't been able to stop herself protesting, remembering the glimpse she had had of the brand new mock-Georgian house she had seen through its encircling protective trees, on the one occasion when Nicholas had driven her past his home.

Personally she would have preferred an older, more established property and certainly she doubted that she would have wanted the frilly festoon blinds and over-decorated rooms she had heard Clarissa describing so enthusiastically to her husband the afternoon she had interrupted their meeting. But Tania accepted fair-mindedly that people had different tastes and ideas.

'Well, they are,' Ann agreed, wrinkling her nose. 'But I suspect that Clarissa stills gets an allowance from James. Certainly she could never afford to run that expensive Mercedes nor to buy all those designer clothes, as well as keeping both boys at such an expensive prep school, if James weren't helping them. I doubt she even knows the meaning of the word "economy". They have a cleaner, and until the boys were at school they had a nanny. No matter how good Nicky's practice is I doubt it runs to financing all that lot, and even the nicest of men must feel the burden of having his wife's step-brother have such a large financial say in their affairs.

'Of course he's tied hand and foot, really. The majority of his business has come to him through James. That's no secret. I don't envy him one iota . . . even if at times I do wonder what it would be like to be able to go out and buy all three of mine new clothes at the same time.'

Ann had laughed unselfconsciously as she made this last statement, causing Tania to warm to her even more. Had she known Ann better she might have been tempted to confide in her and ask her advice, but in the early days after Lucy's birth being independent and showing that she could cope by herself had become such a fierce necessity in her life that she still found it very hard to lean on others, no matter how sympathetic they appeared.

This feeling she had that Nicholas was perhaps being a little more friendly towards her than was strictly necessary was something she would have to deal with on her own.

With a little tact and diplomacy, it should not be too difficult to do so, and, anyway, perhaps she was over-reacting a little, being a touch too sensitive to what was really no more than genuine friend-liness on his part.

He had certainly neither said nor done anything to suggest anything different, and she certainly had far more important things to think about. Such as her shop, for instance.

Another few days and the shop would be opening. She felt her body clench with apprehension and excitement. She had taken extensive advertising in the local Press, and she had timed the opening of her business well, done all she could to ensure its success. The rest was in the lap of the gods and she could only hope that they were disposed to smile kindly on her endeavours.

With one last approving look at the window she turned on her heel and opened the shop door.

She was just about to close it behind her when she saw that a man was about to follow her inside.

For a moment, as she looked into his unsmiling face, a tiny *frisson* of fear ran through her.

He was totally unfamiliar to her, dressed casually in well-worn and very faded blue jeans, and a short-sleeved shirt that acknowledged the heat of the glorious summer they had been enjoying.

His dark hair was untidy and ruffled and he had a smear of oil on one cheekbone. Despite that, he had about him an aura of power and maleness that made her hesitate and then flounder a little before saying quickly, 'I'm sorry, the shop isn't open yet. We don't actually open until Saturday.'

'So I understand.' His voice was cool, slightly abrasive, and very, very controlled, as though he was extremely angry.

She looked at him and discovered that he was. She could see it in the cold greyness of his eyes and the hard set of his mouth.

Her own eyes darkened from hazel to tawny gold in recognition of her apprehension.

'Besides, I haven't come to buy shoes from you, Ms Carter.'

He hadn't? Then what did he want? Was he some kind of local official? Some kind of planning official or someone whom she had unwittingly annoyed?

As she frowned her confusion, she said uncertainly, 'I see. Then...then, why...why have you come to see me?'

'That,' he told her curtly, 'is something I think we can best discuss in privacy.'

Privacy. Her heart pounded. Once, long ago, another man had demanded privacy with her. Lucy had been the result of her acceding to that demand, and, while it was ridiculous to suppose that this man had anything like that in mind, she still could not help the tremor of fear that ran through her, making her tremble visibly.

'I...I'm afraid that's impossible,' she told him huskily. 'You see, I'm just about to collect my daughter...perhaps if I could make an appointment...'

He laughed harshly.

'Oh, yes, that would suit you, wouldn't it? I wonder what's going through that devious head of yours, Ms Carter? Well, I'm sorry, but I don't have any time to waste on conniving females. All I want from you is your assurance that from now on you will cease your relationship with my brother-in-law.'

Tania's mouth dropped. The man had plainly made a mistake...was perhaps even mad. Anger overtook her fear.

'I'm sorry, I can't help you,' she told him crisply. Really, what on earth was he talking about? He must have confused her with someone else. That could be the only explanation for his extraordinary behaviour.

She realised suddenly, her eyes rounding in shocked fascination, that he had produced a cheque-book from the back pocket of his jeans and that he was flicking it open, his mouth curling disdainfully as he derided, 'I see. Well, maybe this will help to convince you. As you see, I've come prepared, Ms Carter. Naturally I didn't expect you to cease your affair out of the goodness of a heart I'm quite sure you don't possess. Shall we say ten thousand pounds?'

'Ten thousand pounds...' She felt sick with shock and pain.

'Not enough? Well, I assure you it's as much as you're going to get.'

Bewilderment gave way to shock and shock to anger as she saw the look of glittering contempt in his eyes.

'Get out of here,' she demanded furiously. 'Just get out before... before I call the police.'

She was speaking wildly, dangerously, her brain warned her. The man was plainly mad. Who knew what on earth he might take it into his head to do if she continued to threaten him?

She was shaking visibly as the adrenalin-fuelled fury pumped through her veins.

'Very clever, but hardly convincing. What exactly will you tell them? That I offered you ten thousand pounds to stop you breaking up my sister's marriage? They'd think I was treating you generously.

This isn't the city where no one gives a damn how his neighbour lives. I'll give you twenty-four hours to think over my offer. After that... Well, let's just say one way or another I'm going to make damn sure you stop trying to wreck my sister's marriage.'

Speechless with shock and fury, Tania watched in silence as he opened the door and left the shop.

She was still standing where he had left her, bathed in an icy sweat of reaction and fear when Ann Fielding walked in with Lucy a few minutes later.

'What on earth was James Warren doing here?' she asked cheerfully as she came in. 'I know he likes to take a sort of patriarchal interest in everything that goes on locally—that comes of being born into the town's founding family, I suppose, but I shouldn't have thought a children's shoe shop would be of much interest to him. Unless...'

She shot Tania a shrewd thoughtful look, and then exclaimed in concern.

'Tania...my dear. Lucy, run upstairs and get your mummy a glass of water, will you? I don't think she's feeling very well.'

Through stiff lips, Tania demanded thickly, 'Just repeat that for me, will you, Ann?'

'Repeat what?' her friend asked in concerned bewilderment.

'Tell me again who it was who just left this shop.'

Anne's frown deepened. 'Tell you... Well, it was James Warren, of course.'

'James Warren.' Tania's soft mouth twisted bitterly. Well, no need to wonder now whose marriage her unwanted visitor had been so passionately defending. Although she still needed to know exactly why he should imagine that she had the slightest interest in either Nicholas Forbes or his marriage. Come to that, if he was so genuinely concerned about preserving his sister's marriage, *she* was the one he ought to talk to, because it was her actions, her behaviour, her habit of publicly and pointedly underlining the differences between her stepbrother and her husband to the latter's disadvantage which was undermining that marriage.

'What's wrong?' Ann pressed her anxiously. 'When I came in you looked so pale. I thought you were going to faint.'

Quickly seizing on the excuse Ann was offering her, Tania agreed tensely.

'Yes. I think it's the heat.'

'Yes, and this is an anxious time for you. I remember what it's like, and from when Tom and I first started up our business. But I'm sure you'll do well, Tania. And if James Warren should take it into his head to make you into one of his pet causes——'

Tania laughed mirthlessly, her lips tight. 'The last thing I want or need is any condescending patronage from someone who believes himself to be the local lord of all he surveys. Thanks for bringing Lucy back for me,' she added curtly, her manner so plainly indicating that she wanted to be on her own that Ann tactfully said her goodbyes and withdrew.

Once she had gone, Tania stood staring into space.

James Warren. So that was Clarissa Forbes all-powerful stepbrother; a very formidable gentleman indeed, but he wasn't going to intimidate her and the next time he came round, making false accusations against her, she was going to let him know in no uncertain terms just how wrong he was.

How dared he imagine...? How dared he suggest...? She frowned quickly. But how had he got the idea that she was in any way other than in a business sense involved with Nicholas?

There was only one way she could find out, and the next time he came round here threatening her she intended to have her own ammunition fully prepared and primed. She would ring Nicholas Forbes and discover just how his brother-in-law had got the false impression that they were having an affair.

And what was more she would do it now, before the heat of her anger cooled and she allowed rationality and caution to take the place of righteous indignation and hot-blooded anger.

CHAPTER TWO

HAVING settled Lucy in their small sitting-room and listened to her happy account of her day, Tania went through into the room she had designated as her 'office' and picked up the telephone.

Nicholas Forbes's secretary sounded uncertain and hesitant when she asked to be put through to him and Tania frowned over this abrupt change in the girl's manner. Normally she sounded breezy and cheerful, and she and Tania had even got to the stage of exchanging the odd few seconds of conversation.

Nicholas, on the other hand, was obviously pleased to hear from her. Prudence forbade her to discuss James Warren's visit with him over the telephone and so she asked instead if he could manage to find the time to call round and see her.

'It is rather urgent, I'm afraid,' she told him.

'No problem. I'll be with you in ten minutes. I was just about to call it a day anyway. Clarissa had a dinner party planned for this evening and I promised her I wouldn't be late. James is just back from the States and so he'll be joining us.'

As she replaced the receiver, Tania reflected that if she had been the one serving him the meal she would have made sure it had a good spoonful of something bitter in it.

How dared he come round here, threatening her, accusing her...leaping to the most preposterous assumptions?

Angrily she paced her small study while she waited for Nicholas to appear.

She had been so looking forward to her new life, so happy about it, and now suddenly, like a dark cloud crossing the sun, that happiness had been blighted. Through no fault of her own she seemed to have fallen foul of the town's most important and influential resident. Well, she didn't care, she decided mentally, tossing her head. Let him do his worst. He was the one who would suffer the most if it ever came out how he had tried to bribe her, a totally innocent person, to give up a non-existent affair with a man who was nothing more than her legal adviser.

Nicholas arrived ten minutes later. Tania let him in through the front of her shop and then led him upstairs to her study.

They had to walk through her sitting-room to get there, and Lucy turned round, beaming when she saw him.

Nicholas was good with children and they responded well to him. Watching him as he listened to Lucy's excited account of her day, Tania felt a small shaft of bitterness lodge itself somewhere deep inside her.

Lucy should have had this as her birthright, should have had a father to whom she could turn with her small pleasures and problems.

Tania had never felt the lack of a man in their lives, but she realised Lucy might feel differently. The absence of her father was a subject which was rarely raised between them. At the large inner city school which she had previously attended, single-parent children had been in the majority, not the minority, and, although Tania had told Lucy as calmly and matter-of-factly as she could the brief circumstances of her conception, editing them so that they could be understood and accepted by a small child, it was as though in some way Lucy had realised it was not a subject her mother cared to discuss and had asked no further questions.

Now, abruptly and painfully, Tania realised that in thinking their lives complete and content she had perhaps been looking at the situation only from her own point of view. It had never struck her before that Lucy might actively miss the presence of a male parent, even though that presence was something she had never experienced.

Now, listening to her laughing and giggling as she responded to Nicholas's gentle teasing, Tania was struck by uncertainty and apprehension.

Was Lucy perhaps secretly nursing a need to have a man in her life? A father?

'What's wrong?' Nicholas asked her with urgent concern once they were alone in her study. 'You sounded worried over the phone.'

'Worried doesn't begin to describe it,' Tania told him tartly. She took a deep steadying breath as she felt the tension build up inside her and then said levelly, 'I had a visit from your brother-in-law this afternoon. He seems to be under the misapprehension that you and I are having an affair and he came here to demand that I stop seeing you. He also offered me ten thousand pounds to do so.'

'Ten thousand!' Nicholas whistled. 'Did you take it?'

Tania stared at him. He was smiling but beneath the smile she could see that he was ill at ease, guilty almost.

'No, I did not. But that isn't why I asked you to come here. What I want to know is why on earth he should imagine that you and I *are* having an affair in the first place, much less attempt to bribe and threaten me into giving you up.'

Nicholas had turned his back on her. He picked up the paperweight on her desk, weighing it absently in his hands, his movements jerky and uncoordinated.

'Nicholas, what is going on?' Tania pressed, reading these betraying signs. 'And please don't tell me you don't know,' she added with dry irony as she removed the paperweight from his hand. 'Because it's perfectly obvious that you do.'

For a moment he was silent and then he shrugged and admitted sheepishly, 'I suppose it's all my fault ... although I never intended—that is, I had no idea that Clarissa would fire James up to such an extent——'

'Just a minute.' Tania stopped him, curtly frowning at him. 'You mean that it's Clarissa who has told her stepbrother that we're having an affair? But what on earth gave her that idea ...? Everyone knows that you're devoted to her and——'

'That's the trouble,' Nicholas interrupted her bitterly. 'I've allowed her to make a doormat out of me for too long. I'm sick and tired of her carping, her criticisms, of being held up to ridicule ... of being made to feel a fool. I've already

told her that if she doesn't love me any more then
we should separate. Even though, for the children's
sake, I feel... Anyway that isn't what she
wants...or so she says. In fact, she got so wrought
up when I suggested it that I began to wonder if I
could perhaps make her jealous, make her believe
that another woman was interested in me...a
woman who didn't despise me or constantly
compare me with another man. She's always had
a very jealous nature...and it's obviously worked
better than I imagined.'

Tania couldn't believe what she was hearing.

'You mean you *deliberately* allowed Clarissa to
believe that you and I are having an affair, even
though there's not the slightest truth in such a suggestion?' she asked, appalled.

Nicholas had the grace to look embarrassed.

'I'd no idea she'd take things so far. I didn't *say*
we were having an affair. I just talked to her about
you, told her how much I admire you... You know
the kind of thing. I had no idea she'd involve James.
I suppose I ought to have done, though. She's
forever running to him with her problems. He's
more important to her than I am——' He broke off,
flushing and biting his bottom lip, and Tania recognised that Clarissa wasn't the only one suffering from jealousy.

Something unpleasant and distasteful stirred deep
inside her at what she was hearing.

'You'll have to tell her the truth,' she announced
flatly. 'And you have to tell your brother-in-law as
well.'

He had gone pale and was avoiding her eyes.

'I will do,' he told her. 'But not just yet. If I can just get her to realise——'

'No,' Tania protested. She was furious with him. How dared he use her like this and without either her knowledge or her consent? 'I can understand that you want to save your marriage,' she told him firmly. 'But I don't believe this is the right way to go about it. What's wrong with simply sitting down and discussing the whole thing honestly with Clarissa? Tell her that you love her and that you resent being compared with her brother. Tell her that you want to make a success of your marriage. After all, you've every incentive to do so, both of you. You must have loved each other when you married . . . you have two beautiful children.'

'One of whom was conceived before we were married,' Nicholas told her, astounding her. 'Oh, *I* wanted to marry her. I was desperately in love with her, but Clarissa . . . Well, I've never been sure whether she married me because she loved me or because she was pregnant. Sometimes I even wonder if Alec is mine. You see, she was involved with another man—a married man—when we first met. She was using me to prevent James from finding out about her affair. He's very strict about such things, very moralistic.'

Tania felt sickened by what she was hearing. Mingled with that sickness was pity for Nicholas, tinged with a little contempt, and as for Clarissa . . .

'You're going to have to tell her the truth, Nicholas,' she insisted curtly. 'Your brother-in-law has given me twenty-four hours in which to make up my mind about his bribe. After that if I refuse to give you up he assured me that he will find some way of making me do so.

'He's a very powerful man locally. I can't afford to have him as my enemy, no matter what my private opinion of a man who accepts the accusations of someone without making the slightest attempt to find out for himself if they're true. I can't help you with your marriage, I'm afraid, and, to be honest with you, if you don't make sure that he knows the truth, then I shall.'

'I'll do my best,' Nicholas told her, 'but it won't be easy convincing Clarissa.'

'Really?' Tania was coldly, icily angry with him now. 'You *do* surprise me. You appeared to have no difficulty in convincing her that we were having an affair. Surely informing her of the truth should be even more easy?'

'I'll do my best,' Nicholas reiterated, but, as she saw him out, Tania wished she could have felt more confident of his determination to make sure Clarissa knew and accepted the true situation between them.

As he got in his car to drive away, she called out urgently to him, 'So you'll make sure she knows everything, won't you, Nicholas?'

The smile he gave her was forced and painful, but she dared not allow herself to waste any sympathy on him. He certainly had not spared a thought for her when he had so recklessly and unwisely involved her without her knowledge in his private affairs.

She had gone from feeling sorry for him for the sad state of his marriage to feeling that perhaps he and Clarissa deserved one another after all. She had nothing but contempt for adults who so cruelly played childish games with one another's emotions.

Surely any good marriage—any worthwhile relationship—demanded total trust, mutual respect, mutual honesty, if that feeling that the human race described as love was going to be allowed a chance to grow to maturity.

If the kind of relationship Nicholas and Clarissa shared was marriage, commitment, then she was glad she had never experienced it.

But then she thought of Lucy, Lucy whom she was perhaps unwittingly denying a very important part of her growing up. Would her daughter as an adult have difficulty in relating to the male sex? Would she have emotional problems and hang-ups because of her lack of a male parent, a male influence in her life?

Uncomfortably she dismissed her thoughts as unproductive, but, later on that evening when Lucy was chatting animatedly about her afternoon at the Fieldings', describing to her how Tom Fielding was making his daughter her very own personalised stencil for decorating her newly painted bedroom walls, she wondered if she was being over-sensitive in detecting a trace of wistful envy in her daughter's voice. Lucy's room in their new flat, while a ten-fold improvement on the claustrophobic and damp room she had occupied in their city tower block, was as yet undecorated. Because of the necessity of opening in time for the autumn term trade in new school shoes, there hadn't been time to do very much as yet with the flat. Once the shop was open and running, then she would be able to turn her attention to making their new home more comfortable.

She had plenty of ideas, plenty of plans, and, determinedly trying to banish James Warren and his threats from her mind, she tried to concentrate instead on discussing with Lucy just how they would decorate her new room.

After Lucy had had her bath and gone contentedly to bed, Tania looked around her sitting-room, mentally giving the plain walls a coat of fresh sunny yellow paint. A pretty stencil frieze around the top of the walls would add a little individuality to the décor; she had taught herself a good many domestic skills over the years, out of necessity more than anything else, and she eyed their comfortable settee she had originally bought second-hand, recognising that it was perhaps time it had a new loose cover, perhaps in a plain damask this time now that Lucy was growing up and the importance of a fabric which would not show every mark was no longer essential. Because her great-aunt had refused to modernise the building in any way, the flat still retained its open fireplaces with their nineteenth-century firebacks.

Worth a fortune now, Ann Fielding had told her enviously, and well worth keeping.

In addition to its two good-sized bedrooms, the sitting-room, the small room she had turned into her study and the bathroom, the flat also had a kitchen-cum-dining-room, but ultimately Tania hoped to extend the rear ground floor of the building to provide Lucy and herself with a down-stairs kitchen with french windows they could open out on to a small courtyard for summer eating.

That, however, was for the future. For the present... Grimly she stared out of her sitting-room window, for once oblivious to the view across the open countryside.

She was furious with Nicholas for involving her in what should have been his strictly private affairs, and how on earth Clarissa could be silly enough to believe his lies about her she really had no idea. The woman must surely realise how much her husband doted on her... but then if she was as jealous as Nicholas had implied, almost pathologically so... Tania frowned. The whole situation repelled her, especially those aspects of it which touched upon Clarissa's relationship with her stepbrother. Clarissa did seem to have an unhealthy dependence on and absorption with her stepbrother.

Surely he, though, as the elder, as the sophisticated and worldly man he was supposed to be, must have long ago recognised the dangers of Clarissa's dependence on him? Surely it should have been up to him to gently ensure that his stepsister turned to her husband to satisfy her emotional needs and not to him? Surely it should have been up to him to gently and painlessly put a proper distance between them...?

Or was she confronting just another example of the male sex's vanity and weakness? Did James Warren perhaps actually relish Clarissa's patent adoration of him, despite Ann's denial of this?

Restlessly she moved away from the window. Twenty-four hours, he had said... In twenty-four hours he would return for her decision. She wondered cynically whether, once he had discovered the truth and his mistake, he would apologise to her for his totally unfounded accusations against her. Privately she doubted it. He simply wasn't the type. She doubted if he had ever admitted to a mistake in his entire life.

She went to bed early, worn out by the events of the day, acknowledging how much strain she was under with the opening of her shop so imminent. She daren't even allow herself to contemplate failure. She had to make a success of this venture. For Lucy's sake if nothing else. She had seen already how much healthier, how much happier her daughter was in their new surroundings. How much less inclined to cling to her.

In many ways it made her heart ache a little that Lucy should be so willing to spend so much time at the Fieldings', but then she reminded herself of how isolated she and Lucy had always been and how much this had worried her in the past. How much she had wanted security, self-confidence, and happiness for Lucy.

It was a long time before she managed to sleep, only to discover in the morning that not only had she overslept but she also had all the signs of an impending migraine.

Mentally cursing James Warren and all his family, she hurried into the bathroom to discover that she was out of the only tablets she had managed to find which, if taken fast enough, sometimes managed to keep her migraine at bay. She knew from painful experience that once she let the headache take hold nothing would take it away.

Luckily there was a chemist in the next street, who listened sympathetically to the reason for her early morning call and thankfully was able to supply her with the drug she needed, although her errand took rather longer than she had anticipated, principally because the chemist was a friendly man who liked to chat with his customers. Once Tania had explained who she was he announced warmly, 'Oh, yes, of course. My wife was saying only the other day that it was a good thing that a decent children's shoe shop had opened up here. She dreads taking our two into the city to kit them out for school. A proper nightmare, she says it is, so I expect you'll be seeing her once you're open.'

As a potential customer Tania felt she could hardly cut him short and risk offending him, with the result that it was almost half an hour before she was able to hurry back to her own shop.

As she went upstairs to the flat, she recognised that it sounded oddly silent. Normally as she opened the door she could hear Lucy humming or talking to herself, but today everywhere was silent.

Her heart started to pound heavily. She had always stressed to Lucy how important it was that she never went anywhere without her; that she never talked to strangers, much less accepted lifts from them, that she never did anything or went with anyone unless she, Tania, had expressly told her beforehand that she might.

Hurrying into the sitting-room, calling her daughter's name, Tania came to an abrupt halt as she discovered a tearful Lucy standing in the kitchen doorway.

'Darling, what is it?' Tania asked anxiously, dropping down on to her knees and gathering her daughter close in her arms, cradling her there.

Where her own hair was conker-red, Lucy's was a slightly lighter colour, more the shade of new chestnuts, silky and burnished, and, unlike her own, Lucy's eyes were grey rather than tawny. Now those grey eyes looked apprehensive and guilty, and as she looked over her daughter's shoulder, Tania saw the scattered shards of china on the kitchen floor.

'I'm sorry. I was just trying to help...'

Tania bit her lip as she recognised one piece of china. As a special treat she had recently given in to a reckless whim and bought a pretty set of breakfast crockery, a real luxury to her since in the past all she had ever been able to afford had been cheap seconds, bought on market stalls.

'I was just trying to make you a cup of tea,' Lucy told her tearfully, 'but the teapot just sort of slipped.'

The teapot. It would have to be that, of course, the most expensive item of the set. But at least it hadn't been full of scalding hot water when Lucy dropped it.

'It doesn't matter,' she said as comfortingly as she could. 'Everyone has accidents.'

And yet, even as she comforted Lucy and told herself that it was after all only a piece of china, she couldn't help grieving for the waste of money its destruction represented. It wasn't that she was mean or penny-pinching, it was simply that she couldn't afford... She sighed faintly to herself. Perhaps it was her own fault... Lucy was just at that stage when she adored 'helping' and being grown-up. She ought to have recognised the danger, ought to have waited a little perhaps before giving in to the impulse towards such extravagance.

*   *   *

It was a day which seemed destined to be fraught with small difficulties and snags, nothing to do, of course, with her own underlying tension and the knowledge that, before it was over, she would once again by confronted by James Warren.

After all, why should she feel apprehensive...? Apprehensive... She laughed bitterly to herself; sick with fear would be a more accurate description of her feelings. Not that she intended to allow him to see it. Hateful man. No, *he* was the one who should be suffering, not her.

She even toyed with the idea of purposely disappearing for the afternoon, but acknowledged this was a cowardly and pointless exercise. She was not playing a point-scoring game against the man. All she wanted was for the situation to be sorted out and the truth revealed so that she could get on with her life and her business, without his unwarranted threats hanging over her.

When after lunch Susan Fielding called round to ask importantly if Lucy would like to go back to her house with her so that they could both watch her daddy making her new stencil, Tania was almost relieved to see her daughter go. Not because she didn't want her company, but she certainly did not want her on hand to witness any confrontation between herself and James Warren.

When three-thirty came and went without any sign of him she told herself with relief that Nicholas must have revealed the truth and, like the bully that he undoubtedly was, James was too embarrassed by his own error to come round and acknowledge the wrong he had done her.

Well, that suited her fine. The last thing she wanted was to see him again. She still felt inwardly bruised and battered from their previous meeting.

It was just gone four o'clock. She was just about to sit down and make herself a cup of tea to wash down the tablets her still-aching head demanded when she heard the shop doorbell ring.

Immediately she knew who it was, but, even knowing, couldn't stop the tension invading her stomach as she walked towards the door and saw James Warren standing on the other side of it.

For a moment she was tempted to leave it locked, but then she noticed that one of her neighbours was watching curiously from the opposite side of the road and so reluctantly she unlocked the door and stepped to one side so that he could walk in.

'Very sensible,' was his jeering comment as he followed her inside. 'Well?' he demanded closing the door behind him. 'I do hope you've made the right decision, because, as I warned you yesterday, I am not prepared to stand by and watch you destroy my sister's marriage.'

Tania stared at him, and then her heart sank. Nicholas hadn't told him the truth—either that or he had told him and he had simply chosen not to believe her.

Tightening her lips, she told him coolly, 'There is no decision for me to make, since I am not having an affair either with your brother-in-law or with anyone else. I don't have affairs, Mr Warren, and, especially, I don't have affairs with married men.'

'No?' His eyebrows rose, his voice dripping with cynicism as he retorted, 'I might be more inclined to believe you if you hadn't already provided the

proof of your own dishonesty by the fact that you
have an illegitimate child, father unknown—or so
you apparently claim.'

The cruelty of it, the sheer ruthless brutality left
her breathless and speechless, her shocked
expression alone betraying to him just how much
damage his words were doing.

When her frozen vocal cords relaxed enough for
her to reply to him, she did so as unemotionally as
she could, her voice low and uneven as she told
him, 'Lucy was conceived when I was eighteen years
old. A very foolish eighteen years old. Eighteen-
year-olds *can* sometimes be foolish and naïve.
Unfortunately, when they're female, that folly can
often have consequences that affect the rest of their
lives.' She ached to be able to throw in his face her
knowledge that his own precious sister had been
carrying a child before she married Nicholas, but
she told herself that she was not going to demean
herself, that she was not going to lower herself to
his level, and, as she held her head high and stared
bitterly at him, she had the satisfaction of seeing
him frown and check before he smiled dangerously
at her.

He said softly, 'I see. Nicholas has been doing a
lot of unburdening of himself to you, hasn't he?
What is it exactly that you're after, Ms Carter? His
money? Without my backing, without the business
I put his way, he'd barely scrape a living. His lifestyle? Again, without my help he couldn't afford
that lifestyle.'

His cynicism stunned her and she reacted to it
instinctively, demanding huskily, 'Couldn't it
simply be Nicholas himself that I want? Just

because your precious sister seems to hold him in
such contempt, it doesn't mean that I feel the same.
In fact, I can't imagine why she's involved you in
this at all. After all, she's scarcely been giving the
impression of a devoted wife, has she? It seems
common knowledge that she prefers your company
to her husband's, that it's to you that she turns for
advice, for companionship, and, of course, for
money,' she added sweetly.

She had the pleasure of seeing his whole face
harden with rage and distaste as he listened to her
taunts.

He didn't like what she was saying to him; he
didn't like it one little bit, but then why should he
expect to be able to stand there and insult her as
much as he wished, without her doing a single thing
to retaliate? Let him see how he liked being insulted,
being accused, being humiliated.

'What exactly is it you're implying?' he demanded savagely, so savagely that immediately
Tania panicked, fear swamping her as he took a
step towards her. She could see the violence in his
eyes, feel it in the heat coming off his body.

'I'm not implying anything,' she told him shakily.
'Nor am _I_ relying on one person's idiotic assumptions and mistaken beliefs to make accusations
which are totally false. The whole town knows that
your precious sister looks not to her husband but
to her brother, that she constantly humiliates
Nicholas by comparing him to you. If he is looking
for affection, for warmth, for love outside his marriage then I doubt that anyone would be surprised.'

'So _that's_ your justification, is it? It's all
Clarissa's fault. Have you forgotten that they have

two children, two children who need both their father and their mother?'

'Just as my daughter needs two parents,' Tania hurled back at him.

'Well, with my ten thousand you'll probably be able to buy yourself a man,' he told her cruelly. 'You *are* going to accept it, aren't you?'

Tania stared at him.

'No,' she told him through clenched teeth. 'No, I am not and what's more I wouldn't accept it if you added another nought to the end and made it one hundred thousand pounds.'

'One hundred thousand. My God, is that your price? Well, let me tell you——'

'No, let me tell you,' Tania interrupted him furiously. 'You come in here, threatening me, bullying me, accusing me. I am not having an affair with Nicholas. And if you don't believe me try asking him.'

'I don't believe you,' he told her flatly. 'And as for asking Nick . . . Well, for your information that was one of the first things I did after I had managed to calm Clarissa's hysterics. Have you any idea what you're doing to my sister? Have you any idea of how delicately balanced her nervous system is? She's always been highly strung, vulnerable where her emotions are concerned.'

'Oh, I'll bet,' Tania muttered under her breath, causing him to break off and glare at her.

'And just what is that supposed to mean?'

Tania had gone way beyond the bounds of common sense or caution now.

'It means,' she told him bitingly, 'that your precious stepsister is one of the most convincing, most machiavellian women I have ever met. And as for her nerves, my bet is that they're made out of re-inforced steel.

'If she's so desperately concerned about her marriage, why doesn't she try behaving like Nicholas's wife? Or is it that both of you prefer the present status quo, where she's married to Nicholas, but where in reality *you're* the most important man in her life?'

Immediately she realised she had gone too far. His mouth went white with rage, his eyes so dark they were almost black.

'My God! How dare you make such a filthy accusation? You... You talk about Clarissa being conniving, when you can sling as much mud as you like, but none of it obscures the fact that you have deliberately set out to destroy my sister's marriage and one way or another I intend to make damn sure you pay for that.'

Tania couldn't believe that he had gone as she sagged against the wall in relief. Her body ached as though it had been kicked, the pounding in her head had reached a sickly crescendo, and her heart was beating so fast she thought she might actually start to hyperventilate.

Calm down, she warned herself, calm down. He's gone... it's over. He's gone...

True, he had threatened her, accused her, frightened her... but what, after all, could he do? She wasn't having an affair with Nicholas. She wasn't having an affair with anyone.

She remembered the insults he had hurled at her and a wave of sickness overwhelmed her.

The stigma attached to Lucy's birth was something she had come to terms with long ago. Most people—the only people she considered worth knowing—were far too generous, far too kind, far too aware to either ask questions about Lucy's birth or to make assumptions.

And she was not the kind to make confidences, to explain or excuse herself. She had made a simple error of judgement. She had looked for love and found only lust. She had behaved foolishly, irresponsibly, but she had been very young, very naïve, and, from the viewpoint of eleven years on, she could feel only compassion and sorrow for the girl she had been then.

If James Warren chose to revile her for that childhood mistake, that error of judgement which had led to Lucy's conception, then let him. It only confirmed her view that he was simply not a man she cared to know, and, one day, she promised herself, she would give him the pleasure of telling him so.

She after all had as much right to live in this town as he. Her roots—or at least those connected with her great-aunt's predecessors—were buried deep here too.

Her inheritance, her new business . . . these were her chances to make a better life for Lucy and herself and she intended to do just that. Nothing, no one—much less a man like James Warren—was going to prevent her from doing so.

CHAPTER THREE

'NERVOUS?'

Tania gave Ann Fielding a tense smile.

'Yes. Does it show?'

'Only a little,' Ann reassured her.

In precisely half an hour's time she would be opening the shop doors to the small but important gathering of local dignitaries and media people who had been invited to the pre-opening cocktail party which Ann had insisted was *de rigueur* if her business was to gain the maximum support and publicity.

She had objected that the cost of such an exercise must surely outweigh its benefits but Ann had overruled her firmly, insisting that it was essential.

She certainly hoped it would prove a worthwhile investment. Nicholas had laughed at her when he'd discovered she intended to prepare the refreshments herself.

'Why not have them catered?' he had suggested. 'Clarissa uses a very good local firm.' This apparently consisted of two girls she had gone to school with who had set up in business doing business lunches, dinner parties and the like, but Tania had shaken her head, protesting that it would be a wasteful extravagance.

When Ann Fielding had learned what she was intending to do she had fully approved.

'Why don't you let me give you a hand?' she suggested. 'I did a cordon bleu course in the early days of our marriage, before Tom persuaded me that my artistic talents would be of more use setting up the shop, and advising our customers on their décor.'

She said it with a grin, but Tania wasn't deceived. Ann was very artistically talented indeed and Tania had marvelled at her interior design skills when she had first been shown round their home. She was not surprised that Tom found his wife a very valuable asset when it came to adding those all-important decorative touches to a client's colour scheme.

It had been Ann who had gently suggested her present window dressing, adding that she knew just the place where they could find suitable birch branches, which later on could be sprayed with mock 'snow' for Christmas and decorated with masks for Halloween.

Now, Tania surveyed the buffet 'table', which in reality comprised a couple of trestles and some planks borrowed from Tom, covered in a pair of old sheets to disguise them, with home-made garlands of dried flowers decorating the table front, their colours in keeping with the rich autumn shades of her stock.

Cleverly Ann had even suggested food on a similar colour theme, laughing at Tania's awe, and explaining gently, 'You'll soon learn. Especially when you discover how much cheaper it is to do these things yourself rather than hire an expensive window dresser, and eye-appeal does make all the difference. I couldn't believe the number of commissions we got one spring when I decorated our main window as a nursery complete with hand-painted mobiles and nursery rhyme scenes painted on the walls. It was one of our most adventurous schemes, and one that brought in the most profit.

'Never underestimate the amount of money parents are prepared to spend on their children, especially when it comes to doing the right thing for their future health and development, and then, of course, at Christmas you're bound to have plenty of doting aunts and grannies who just can't resist buying their little darlings a pair of patent shoes or some cute little baseball boots.'

Ann was undoubtedly very shrewd and practical when it came to retailing and Tania was grateful for all the help she was giving her, but even so she could not bring herself to confide in her new friend and admit what had happened with James Warren.

Was it because of her habitual and instinctive need to remain independent, a need that sprang from a very real fear that once she gave in to the need to lean on someone else, no matter how briefly, she would never again be able to find the strength to stand alone; or was it because she was afraid that Ann might not believe her?

Uncomfortable with such deep and potentially destructive thoughts, she tried to concentrate on the buffet table.

A glass of wine, something to eat that had more eye-appeal than actual substance, the feeling that people were privileged to be asked to attend her opening, these were the things that would make her pre-opening party a success with her guests and guarantee her the extra publicity she needed, Ann told her, and certainly looking at her stock-room, for this evening transformed with clever shadowed lighting and the discreet hanging of various fabrics into a cosy 'drawing-room', there was no reason why the evening should not be a success.

Ann had even persuaded her to buy herself a new dress for the occasion; a ridiculous extravagance but one which Ann assured her would more than pay for itself.

Another important tip, she had insisted, when she had dragged Tania off to the town's small exclusive parade of boutiques, calmly depositing her own children and Lucy in Tom's care.

'Look rich when you're poor. It's essential. Only the rich can afford to dress badly and look shabby. Here,' she had added, removing a dress from one of the rails, 'try this.'

When Tania had eyed what looked like little more than a tubular hand of golden bronze stretch jersey with distaste and doubt, Ann had laughed at her and insisted, 'It will look wonderful on you, believe me. I know. And the colour is just right both for your colouring and for the season.'

Much to Tania's astonishment, Ann had been proved right. The jersey, once on, had proved to have a simple elegance that justified its exorbitant price ticket.

'You'll more than get your money's worth out of it,' Ann had promised her. 'Once the season gets into full swing, you'll find you'll be wearing it again and again.'

'The season?' Tania had queried, perplexed.

'The dinner party season,' Ann had explained, with a grin. 'We're a sociable lot round here. We have to be, after all. It's up to us to provide our own entertainment. Apart from the local Chamber of Commerce affairs which you'll be invited to attend, there'll be a whole host of small dinner parties, plus larger more casual affairs for Halloween, Bonfire Night. You mention it, we celebrate it.'

'Oh, but I couldn't. Lucy...'

'Lucy can sleep over with Susan,' Ann had told her cheerfully, sweeping aside her objections. 'Tom's sister's eldest girl is studying for A levels and glad of all the baby-sitting money she can get. She's a sensible girl, too. Not the kind you'd fear to leave with even the smallest child.'

'Mmm. I'm glad you went ahead and got the earrings,' Ann commented now, studying Tania's appearance. 'That brief glint of gold when you move your head just sets off the rest of your appearance. Not to mention the fact that it adds a very glamorous touch of mystery and allure.

'I suspect you'll find more than one father is going to be escorting his offspring into your shop over the next few weeks.'

She stopped laughing when she saw Tania's expression, touching her arm lightly, 'What's wrong?'

'I'm not interested in married men. I never have been and I never will be,' Tania told her shortly, adding, almost under her breath, 'In fact I'm not interested in men, period.'

'I'm sorry. I didn't mean to offend you. Of course I never meant to imply——'

'Oh, it's all right,' Tania told her. 'I'm just feeling a bit raw and sensitive at the moment.' She bit her lip, wondering if perhaps after all she should not confide in Ann and ask her advice, but then Susan and Lucy came bustling into the room, eyeing the buffet table enviously.

Ann said firmly, 'Now, you two, you both know we've made up special plates of treats for your supper provided you both behave well, and stay upstairs.'

'Yes, and I'm going to sleep in Lucy's bedroom tonight, aren't I? I'm going to sleep in the top bunk because I'm the eldest,' Susan announced importantly. 'And I'm going to help Lucy think up a stencil for Daddy to make for her.'

Over their head Tania gave Ann an embarrassed look.

'I'm so sorry,' she apologised afterwards. 'I'll explain to Lucy that she can't expect Tom to make her a stencil.'

'Of course he'll make her one,' Ann assured easily. 'And, what's more, you and I will paint it on her walls.'

'I've already accepted so much help from you,' Tania protested shakily. 'I really feel——'

'Well, don't,' Ann cut in. 'After all, that's what life is all about, isn't it? Helping others, passing on kindnesses and favours...and besides, this relationship with your Lucy is good for Susie. With being the youngest and the only girl she's tended to be a little too docile and dependent. I'm only too delighted to see her coming out of herself and trying to boss Lucy around,' she chuckled. 'Now, we've got exactly ten minutes before they start to arrive. And I suggest we use it to dose those butterflies of yours with a large glass of wine...'

Perhaps it was the wine, perhaps it was the relief, perhaps it was simply the warmth and kindness she could feel radiating out towards her from the people around her, Tania reflected an hour later as she allowed herself to acknowledge the almost beatific state of happiness which she was experiencing.

Everyone had been complimentary about her new venture, promising support and patronage. Her window display had been admired, her buffet eaten, her wine drunk. The reporter from the local paper had promised to do an item on her, adding that she would certainly bring both her girls in for their school shoes.

'They're just at that age when they loathe anything of which I approve,' she confided. 'So I'll probably have to bribe them into accepting a pair of sensible, suitable-for-school shoes with something a little more acceptable for going out.'

'I think we've got the very thing,' Tania assured her, mentally reviewing her stock.

She had anticipated that people would stay for an hour at the most but as yet no one was showing any signs of wanting to leave and she was glad that Ann had persuaded her to buy in those extra bottles of wine.

Totally absorbed in her duties as hostess and in her anxiety for the success of her business, she was completely unaware of how much she herself was attracting people's attention.

Normally she dressed for warmth and practicality and so she was oblivious to the fact that her slender elegant figure was causing quite a stir among her male guests.

Others weren't, though, and more than one woman noticed approvingly that, although Tania was stunningly attractive with the unfair added advantage of a gorgeous figure, she was plainly not the kind of woman who intended to capitalise on her looks, and that she seemed to prefer female company to male. Approvingly they decided that they need have no qualms about including her in their social circles, dismissing their initial wariness when they had discovered the newcomer was an unmarried woman of twenty-nine with a ten-year-old daughter.

Everyone was entitled to one mistake, was the general consensus of opinion, and those rogue males who had attended the party, in the hope that Tania might be the kind of woman who enjoyed indulging in the odd emotionless sexual adventure, soon realised that such hopes were in vain.

The only person who had not put in an appearance at her party was Nicholas, which in the circumstances was hardly surprising. Naturally he would not want to add fuel to Clarissa's fire by attending the party and Tania was quite frankly relieved by his absence.

And then some second sense made her look up just as the shop door opened and three people walked in.

She felt the blood clog in her veins as she recognised Clarissa's diminutive figure in between those of her husband and her stepbrother.

She was clinging equally grimly to both dark-suited arms, her face set in petulant, bitter lines as she said loudly, 'Honestly, Nicky, I don't know why you insisted on bringing us here. Poor James will be bored out of his mind. I mean, what on earth interest is some poky little shoe shop to us?'

Everyone had gone silent, but, instead of being embarrassed, Tania found that she was actually coldly angry. Very angry.

'Nicholas,' she said smoothly stepping forward to welcome him, 'And you've brought your wife...'

Her tone indicated that Clarissa's presence wasn't entirely welcome or expected, bringing a dark flush of anger to the blonde's face.

'Tania, this is James——'

'Yes, I've already met your brother-in-law,' Tania interrupted him carelessly, deliberately turning her back on James. 'I'm afraid there's hardly any food left, although we can probably rustle up a glass of wine.'

Again she allowed her voice to indicate that it was immaterial to her how affronted or offended they might feel at this offhand hospitality.

'Oh, come on, Nicky,' Clarissa raged immediately, her voice thin and whiney. 'Don't let's stay. It's the most dreary affair,' she added spitefully, glaring at Tania.

Nicholas flushed but stood his ground. 'You go if you want to, darling,' he suggested quietly. 'But I rather think I should stay. Tania *is*, after all, a client.'

Tania held her breath, recognising immediately what he was trying to do, and wishing that he had chosen anyone but her with whom to arouse Clarissa's jealousy.

Indeed she was so cross with him that she darted him an indignant sparkling look which was bodily intercepted by James who stepped between them, saying coolly, 'Since we *are* here, it would be churlish of us to leave without at least inspecting Ms Carter's wares.'

He was, Tania knew, being deliberately insulting. She felt her skin burn as his glance slid slowly and deliberately over her body, whilst Clarissa said gleefully and maliciously, 'Oh, I doubt she's got anything to offer that would interest you, James. James is used to only the very best...of everything,' she told Tania nastily.

Tania stared at her. She was almost shaking with fury. Behind her she was aware of people's covert interest and was only thankful that at least they could not overhear what was being said.

'Really?' she responded acidly. 'You *do* surprise me.'

She had the pleasure of seeing Clarissa's mouth drop open. James Warren's spoilt stepsister obviously wasn't used to people fighting back, she reflected grimly. She was so used to using her stepbrother as a shield—a battering ram—that she thought she could hand out her insults with impunity.

'Nicholas, perhaps you'd help yourself to wine,' Tania suggested coolly. 'I must go and attend to my other guests.'

She turned away from them and was astounded when Nicholas reached out and placed one hand on her arm.

'You're looking very lovely tonight,' he told her softly, but not so softly that his wife and his brother-in-law could not hear.

Tania was furious with him. She pulled her arm away and hissed under her breath. 'Stop it, Nicholas. Save your compliments for your wife, if you don't mind!' But it was already too late. Clarissa was glaring at her with venom and fury, while James was regarding her in a way that made her heart drop like a high-speed lift wrenched free of its moorings.

In the end the unwelcome trio stayed just a little longer than half an hour, and, although Tania did as much as she could to keep as great a distance between them as possible, she could feel James Warren's concentration on her. It created a prickle of unpleasant tension at the base of her neck and made her ache to turn round to see if he actually *was* watching her or if she was simply imagining it, but she refused to give in to her need or to give him the satisfaction of knowing how much his appearance had upset her.

He had threatened her and, despite her innocence, she *was* afraid of him, she recognised. It was almost as though the power that emanated from him reminded her in some deep-rooted psychological way of the physical power Lucy's father had used against her when he'd compelled her to have sex with him.

It wasn't that she feared James Warren in the sexual sense. Clarissa had been right about one thing, she reflected grimly as she tried to concentrate on the conversation going on around her. James Warren would certainly curl up his fastidious mouth at the very suggestion that he might want any kind of sexual intimacy with a woman like her. No, it was a different kind of fear: the protective fear of a mother for her child when she knows that child's security is threatened, the very natural fear of any human being when it knows it is weaker than its aggressor.

She was afraid that somehow he would make good his threat and destroy everything she was trying to build here, and, no matter how much she assured herself that he wasn't God, that he wasn't omnipotent, it wasn't until the three of them had actually quitted the shop that she felt able to release a shaky breath of relief.

'Well, I never imagined you'd get a visit from James,' Ann told her admiringly. 'Of course he *does* tend to take a patriarchal interest in everything that goes on locally. Even so...'

They were on their own. Everyone else had gone but Ann had insisted on staying behind to help Tania clear up.

'Clarissa and Nick didn't seem too happy, did they?' she gossiped cheerfully as she gathered up the used glasses. 'Mind you, I'm not surprised. He

should never have married her. She's far too spoilt,
and I doubt that she ever really loved him. It seems
such a shame, though. She ought to be idyllically
happy—a good, generous husband, those two lovely
boys, a beautiful home . . .'

'And a doting stepbrother, who's prepared to step
in and wave his magic wand whenever necessary,'
Tania suggested acidly, causing Ann to frown and
then grin.

'I think you've got your characters mixed up. It's
the fairy godmother who has the wand, isn't it?
Although, I grant you, James has been very generous with her, which can't really help poor Nick.
James Warren would be a hard act for any man to
live up to.'

'Really? Of the two of them I prefer Nicholas,'
Tania said curtly, and then bit her lip as she saw
Ann's astonishment. What on earth was she doing?
Comments like that could only add dangerous fuel
to the fire Nicholas had so stupidly lit under her.

'You *do*?' Ann was plainly astonished. 'I think
we've got all the glasses now. Shall I wash?' she
suggested, mercifully changing the subject.

CHAPTER FOUR

AT THE end of the week, the morning before her shop was due to open, when a very good piece appeared about her venture in the local paper, Tania recognised the wisdom of Ann's insistence on her pre-opening party, and generously she said as much when she and Ann were discussing the newspaper piece over a cup of coffee.

'Yes, it *is* good, isn't it? Well, let's keep our fingers crossed that your potential customers will be equally impressed. By the way, I wanted to have a word with you about the girls. They'll both start back at school soon. How about me taking them both and collecting them in the afternoon for the first week? Just to give you time to get on your feet. I think that Lucy feels happy enough with us now not to feel that you're neglecting her in any way.

'Once you've seen how the business is going to work, we can make some other arrangements. Our two are the only ones attending school from here, so I'm afraid it isn't a chore we can share with anyone else.'

'That would be great, if you're sure you don't mind. I'm going to have to think about how I can work things so that I can get Lucy to and from school, and it's been something that's been worrying me. In the morning it isn't so bad, but I can hardly close the shop for an hour in the afternoon while I collect her, and as for letting her come home on her own, these days...

'Quite,' Ann agreed, adding firmly, 'I don't even allow the boys to come home on their own, although both of them are beginning to pester me to allow them to ride their bikes to school. Perhaps next year in the summer when we've got the light evenings back... You never feel you can do the right thing by them, do you? Too much protection and you feel you're smothering them, not allowing them to grow and develop; too little and... Well, it's every parent's nightmare, isn't it? And every time you open a paper these days, you're confronted by the reality of children's vulnerability.

'By the way, I don't know if you've had any thoughts about it yet, but if you find you need a Saturday girl I'd like to suggest my niece. She's helped us out in the past, and I can recommend her. She's a sensible girl, intelligent, pleasant.'

'It is something I've been considering,' Tania agreed. 'But I want to see how business goes first.'

They parted ten minutes later when Ann announced that it was her day for doing her large supermarket shop. She groaned as she picked up her jacket.

'I dread it.'

'Me too,' Tania agreed. 'And I always end up with a trolley which has four wheels that all want to go in opposite directions.'

After Ann had gone, she reread the article, but the warm glow of elation it gave her soon faded as her mind returned to the unpleasant scene with Nicholas and his family.

She could understand his feelings, but she wished he had thought of using someone else to bait his trap with. Surely Clarissa must have girlfriends whom he could equally effectively have used? Maybe he could even have persuaded one of them to play along with him in the knowledge that ultimately they would be helping their friend's marriage to grow and strengthen.

This involvement in someone else's life was a complication she just didn't want. Especially when it was going to bring her into confrontation with James.

At the party, when he had looked at her in that cold, contemptuous way, his eyes bleak and grim, she had been surprised to discover just how unpleasant his cold-eyed scrutiny had felt. She tried to shrug the knowledge aside.

It was true that it was unusual for her to react so intensely to a stranger's opinion of her. She had learned very young to cut herself off from the negative emotions of others. She had had to when she was pregnant with Lucy. She had been subjected to so much disapproval then, so much anger and criticism.

The authorities, no doubt with mainly altruistic motives, and in the knowledge of the problems ahead of her, had tried to persuade her to have Lucy adopted. She well remembered the anger and disbelief which had taken the place of the earlier avuncular if slightly condescending kindness of her male doctor when she had refused to accept his advice. She would be facing many many problems if she went ahead and brought Lucy up alone and she would be facing them alone, he had warned her severely. She had remained stubbornly silent, reflecting that she was used to facing life's problems on her own and that he was wrong. She would not be alone. She would have her child.

Perhaps the attitudes she had come across then had left a message indelibly printed across her brain that other people's disapproval was something she must learn to live with. Certainly she was not used to reacting to it in the way she was reacting to James Warren's.

Was it perhaps because she knew she was being unjustly accused, that his opinion of her was completely erroneous and unfounded? But why should that bother *her*? He wasn't a man she knew or was likely to know in any personal sense. He wasn't anyone who was likely to play an important role in her life, so his opinion of her whether good or bad scarcely merited the mental attention she was giving it.

Was she really afraid that as someone of importance locally he could if chose adversely affect the success of her business?

Yes, that was probably it, she told herself thankfully. It was silly to allow herself to feel that her feelings were involved on a more personal level, that his disapproval touched upon her deepest-held convictions about herself as a human being, as a woman... That in falsely accusing her he was someone leaving her defiled emotionally in the same way that Lucy's father had left her feeling defiled physically.

She had long ago come to accept that while her one and only sexual experience had been unpleasant it was not necessarily indicative of the attitude of the entire male sex. In fact whenever she came across a couple like Ann and Tom she discovered within herself a small ache of regret that fate had not allowed her the time to discover that the world held men who treated their sexual partners with respect and generosity. Lucy's birth and her struggle to support them both had left her with neither the time nor the inclination to admit anyone else to their small and enclosed world.

For a long time she had been highly suspicious of all men, and then by the time she had grown through that and occasionally allowed herself to accept the odd date with the men who asked her out she had been wary of allowing herself to get involved, having seen the effect of any such often temporary relationships on the children of other single mothers.

She didn't want that kind of pain for Lucy. She didn't want *her* daughter giving her love and trust to some man, substituting him for the father she had never known, only to have to go through the trauma of losing him when his relationship with Tania came to an end. And pleasant though her odd dates had been there had never been anything about the men concerned to make her want to continue the relationship.

She had long ago come to the conclusion that she had a very low sex drive, or that she had been so traumatised by Lucy's conception that her natural female instincts had been effectively cauterised.

Occasionally, though, when she was watching a film or reading a book, something in the relationship between the two lovers would affect her so deeply that she was left with a tiny ache of pain and loneliness, an indistinct longing for something she had never personally experienced but which she knew instinctively must exist.

That was natural enough and acceptable if somewhat uncomfortable. What galled her now though was that there had been a moment, a second or so, the briefest span of time the other night when she had looked at James Warren, had unwittingly focused on the shape and curve of his mouth and for some reason had experienced the shattering discovery that there was a dangerous and perverse curiosity inside her to experience the sensation of that hard mouth moving against her own.

She had shut herself off from such thoughts immediately, physically taking a step back from her antagonist as she fought to subdue her shocked outrage.

It was almost in some way as though he had practised black magic against her and put those thoughts into her mind against her will.

And yet when she recalled them now there was still that tiny involuntary curl of sensation in the pit of her stomach, that unwanted and far too enlightening pulse of awareness. How *could* she feel desire for a man like James Warren? Had her body run mad?

Firmly telling herself that what she was experiencing was undoubtedly some kind of hormonal aberration, some kind of reaction to the stress and anxiety of these last weeks which had found a focus in James Warren because of his threats against her, she reminded herself that she had work to do, and that the order which had arrived this morning still had to be unpacked and stored away, and that, moreover, she had promised herself that she would spend the afternoon with Lucy.

She had planned to take her for a walk. The fresh air would do them both good.

She wasn't sure whether to feel chagrin or amusement later in the day when she informed Lucy of her plans and got an unenthusiastic response.

'I *was* going to go round and play with Susan,' Lucy objected.

'You can play with her tomorrow,' Tania reminded her. So much for her fears that Lucy might be beginning to feel resentful of the time the shop was demanding and neglected because of it.

'Susan goes swimming every Friday night,' Lucy informed her wistfully. 'They all go. Mr Fielding takes them. I expect he'd take me too.'

'Not this week,' Tania told her firmly. 'If you want to go swimming you and I could go this afternoon.'

'It's not the same,' Lucy told her. 'There won't be anyone there for me to play with.'

Telling herself that her daughter was still very much in the honeymoon stage of her new friendship, and that surely after a while she would cease to compare everything Susan's family did with their own lifestyle to its detriment, Tania suggested pacifyingly, 'Well, we'll go for a walk instead, shall we? We haven't had much time to explore yet, have we?'

She had already bought a local map with all the public footpaths marked on it.

It was a warm day with the leaves just beginning to turn, a reminder of the dry summer they had had, Tania reflected later as she and Lucy got out of the car and headed for their chosen footpath.

The local conservation society was keen to keep the local footpaths open and well used, Ann had informed her, and here on the edge of the town was a small and very tidy parking area with a very clear map of the locality and its footpaths.

The one Tania had chosen followed the path of the river and then cut across a couple of fields, bringing them back to their starting point.

Although initially Lucy had been unenthusiastic about their walk, once they set out she soon began to chatter happily, asking a dozen or more questions in the first ten minutes, causing Tania to stop and consult her local guide so that she could answer them.

It was Lucy who first spotted the otter as he swam towards his nest in the riverbank, her delight in their sighting of the sleek, playful creature banishing her earlier sulks.

In the distance, half a mile or so from the riverbank, almost hidden in an encircling band of trees, stood a house with tall twisted chimneys. Through the turning leaves Tania could see the rosy glow of its brick walls and she sighed a little enviously, recognising the age and charm of the building.

It looked a perfect family home. Old and rambling, but not too large; perhaps originally it had been a small manor house or a prosperous farm. She was just wondering idly about its past when Lucy tugged on her arm and said eagerly, 'Look, Mum.'

A liver and white spaniel was rushing excitedly towards them along the footpath.

Lucy, who loved dogs, hurried eagerly towards it, and while dog and child recognised one another in mutual approval and delight, Tania heard a stern male voice calling firmly, 'Rupert, here...'

She froze as she recognised it, her body tense and alert even before James Warren strode round the corner and stopped abruptly.

'I'm sorry,' he began to apologise curtly, halting as he recognised her. 'Rupert is inclined to behave badly at times. I hope he didn't alarm you.' Polite words—but that was all they were.

He stopped speaking, his frown lifting as Lucy put her arm around the dog and whispered enviously, 'Isn't he lovely, Mum. I wish we had a dog.'

Tania sighed. They had been through this in the past. Then it had been impossible for them to own a dog, but now... Maybe in the spring when she knew how the business was going, and things were a little more settled, but it would have to be a more placid breed than this attractive but quite obviously scatty spaniel.

'You like dogs, do you?' James was asking Lucy, squatting down beside her and giving her a smile of such warmth that for some reason Tania felt as though she had been suddenly left outside a special and very charmed circle. He would never smile at her like that, she recognised bleakly, and then bit her lip, worrying at it physically in the way her brain was worrying at the danger of such a line of thought.

When she stepped forward and said briskly, 'Come along, Lucy, we don't want to delay Mr Warren,' her voice was more curt than she had intended.

Lucy looked up at her, puzzled and a little hurt at being so summarily dragged away from her new friends.

The spaniel seemed equally reluctant to depart, turning huge mournful eyes in Lucy's direction and giving a tiny, wistful howl.

'Definitely a case of love at first sight,' James Warren murmured drily to her.

'Then it's a love-affair that's doomed to be blighted, isn't it?' Tania told him bitingly.

His eyebrows rose. He studied her for a moment in a rather disconcerting manner and then said in a clipped voice, 'I'm delighted if somewhat surprised that you appear to think so. This dog belongs to Nicholas, or rather to his sons. I'm merely exercising him for Clarissa and trying to instil some manners in him, since her husband doesn't appear to have the time to do so. But perhaps now that you appear to have taken my advice Nicholas will be spending a little more time with his wife and family.'

Tania stared at him. Did he *really* believe she was the kind of woman who would be impressed by his . . . his threats . . . ? Did he really believe that if she had actually committed herself to Nicholas she would allow *him* to change her mind?

Too angry to respond to him, she called abruptly to Lucy, waiting while her daughter disentangled herself from the spaniel and then quickly hurrying her back along the path before she could give vent to the emotions boiling up inside her.

'Who was that, Mum?' Lucy insisted on asking her once they were out of sight of both James and the dog.

'He's James Warren,' Tania told her. 'Nicholas's brother-in-law.'

'I liked him,' Lucy told her, adding coaxingly, 'I liked Rupert too. Mum, do you think now that we're living here and—— ?'

'We'll see,' Tania interrupted her firmly, knowing quite well what was coming. 'A dog is a big responsibility, Lucy. Once you've settled at school and we've seen how the shop's coming along, then we can think about taking on a puppy.'

She had always had a policy of wherever possible explaining her decisions to Lucy and never simply stating them without any explanation. Now she was rewarded with a faint sigh but with Lucy's genuine acceptance of her decision.

'How's it going? I've left the girls with Tom and the boys are playing football. I'm supposed to be in charge of the shop, but I've slipped out for a few minutes just to see how you're doing. Whoops! Better leave you to it.' Ann laughed as a customer came up to Tania firmly dragging a small dungaree-clad child with her.

The shop had been open for three hours, and so far Tania had been busier than she had hoped or expected.

There had been a constant stream of people in the shop, most of them serious buyers rather than browsers, all of them expressing delight and approval when she was able to offer them a selection of the kind of shoes for which they were looking.

More than one mother ended up buying not only a pair of sensible, sturdy school shoes for her child, but a pair of the attractive and equally well-fitting continental 'fashion' footwear that Tania had taken a gamble on stocking.

Although inclined to be expensive, this footwear had a bright stylishness which couldn't fail to appeal to her young customers.

If this present rush continued her only problems were going to be restocking and finding another pair of hands to help her take care of her customers, Tania reflected, as Ann reminded her that she was available to take over for an hour or so at lunchtime if Tania felt she needed a break.

Tania doubted that she would; so far she felt as though she was riding a wave of boundless energy and excitement, fuelled no doubt by the constant procession of eager customers in and out of the shop.

At twelve o'clock Ann arrived as she had promised. The shop was still full and she signalled to Tania that she would wait, when she realised that Tania was dealing with a customer.

The woman had just paid her bill and was on the point of departing with her purchases when the shop door opened, and when she looked up Tania saw Clarissa Forbes walking in, accompanied by two boys who were obviously her sons.

Watching discreetly as Clarissa prowled aggressively round the shop, disturbing the displays and disparaging her stock in a voice which Tania suspected was deliberately intended to carry, Tania felt her stomach muscles clench in a mixture of anger and dread.

Eventually Clarissa sat down, but Tania was already dealing with an enquiry from a rather harassed woman who was nervously asking if she could possibly recommend a good shoe for her daughter that cost under thirty pounds.

It was obvious that the other woman was not well off and moreover that she felt uncomfortable, and, remembering her own days of pinching and scraping, of wanting to do her best for Lucy and yet knowing she had such limited resources, Tania was deliberately kind and reassuring as she explained that she was carrying a range of very good children's shoes which were reasonably priced and yet which at the same time paid attention to such important details as fitting and width.

Out of the corner of her eye, she could see Clarissa growing increasingly impatient, but she refused to allow herself to be affected by her rudeness.

Ann, realising what was happening, stepped forward to try and help Clarissa, but she said rudely, 'No, you can't help me. What do *you* know about fitting shoes? I want the manageress.'

Even the way she described her was somehow derogatory, Tania seethed, when she was eventually free to go over and ask how she could help.

She was half prepared for it, when, after insisting on trying virtually every style in the shop, much to her two sons' obvious embarrassment, Clarissa announced loudly that she had nothing of anything like a suitable quality.

Behind her Tania heard the shop door open, and Clarissa, who was facing it, bent down and picked up a pair of shoes which had been left there by a previous customer and which were obviously not the right size for either of her two boys, and before Tania could stop her, she insisted on trying to cram one of them on to her elder son's feet, crying out shrilly, 'Oh, for heaven's sake, you stupid woman, anyone can see that it won't fit. Really, this is ridiculous . . . I thought you people were supposed to be properly trained.' She got to her feet, sweeping aside several shoe boxes, her face set in tight lines of anger as she exclaimed, 'James, it's no use. We'll have to go to Chester. I know you believe in patronising local business, but this woman is so inefficient.'

The shop was busy with potential customers. Tania knew that her face was flushed with anger and embarrassment, and the very last thing she needed was to discover that James Warren was standing right behind her, silently observing his stepsister's horrible behaviour.

Just for a minute, Tania found that she was trembling on the verge of losing her temper and telling him just exactly how disruptive Clarissa was trying to be, and then she recognised that it would be a complete waste of time, that he would be bound to support his stepsister, to encourage her even.

Ignoring Tania, frowning slightly as he took in the whole scene, James Warren enquired firmly, 'Where's Nicholas? I thought *he* was going to take you and the boys out today.'

'Oh, you know Nicky,' Clarissa said spitefully. 'He's far too busy to bother with us. And as to where he is, why don't you ask Ms Carter here? I'm sure she has far more idea than I.'

Aware of the amount of speculation and curiosity they were attracting, Tania said, as quickly and neutrally as she could, 'I'm sorry if we can't help you, Mrs Forbes.'

But it was obviously the wrong thing to do, because, as James extended his hand towards her, Clarissa turned to Tania and hissed bitterly, 'Oh, I'll just bet you are. Just as you're *sorry* that you're having an affair with my husband.'

Tania gasped, unable to stop herself, thankful that no one else appeared to have overheard Clarissa's whispered jibe. No one else apart from James Warren, that was, who was now regarding her with cold dislike.

'It's no good, James. She's absolutely refused to give him up,' Clarissa told her stepbrother. There were tears in her eyes, her face a tragic mask of pain and misery. If she hadn't known better, Tania might almost have felt genuine pity for her. She opened her mouth to announce that she had said no such thing and then closed it again.

She was not going to get embroiled. She was not going to lower herself to their level. She was not going to be contaminated by their lies and deceit.

She stared proudly, haughtily almost at James, challenging him with her gaze.

For a moment she thought he was going to retaliate; to say something, make another threat perhaps, but, to her astonishment and relief, he seemed to change his mind, touching Clarissa firmly on the arm and drawing her away towards the door.

Instinctively Tania followed them there, anxious for them to be gone, and then wished she hadn't as James opened the door for Clarissa and his nephews and then turned to her and said emotionlessly, 'It seems you're determined to ignore my warnings. I only hope you're fully prepared to meet the consequences, and, while you're thinking about that, perhaps you might spare a thought for them as well,' he suggested grimly, nodding in the direction of the two young boys.

Tania pressed her lips together, willing herself to bite back the retorts clamouring for utterance. What was the use of attempting to defend herself? He wouldn't believe her. He wouldn't *want* to believe her.

She turned back to the shop, firmly going forward to attend to another customer, refusing to allow herself to give in to the shaky *malaise* that was pervading her.

Only when the shop was finally empty did Ann finally come across and ask anxiously, 'What on earth was all that about?'

Tania was too exhausted to dissemble.

'Clarissa Forbes thinks I'm having an affair with Nicholas,' she told her tiredly.

'She thinks *what*?'

Ann was so plainly astounded, so plainly disbelieving that Tania felt a little of the heaviness of her burden lift.

'Ridiculous, isn't it,' she agreed. 'He's my solicitor, that's all.'

'Well, if I were James I'd be seriously concerned about that sister of his,' Ann said roundly. 'She's always been inclined to jealousy, especially where James is concerned, but to leap to that kind of assumption with nothing to back it up... She's always been the highly strung type, given to hysterics and dramatics.'

'It isn't entirely her fault,' Tania felt bound to say, suddenly feeling a need to unburden herself. 'Nicholas is partly to blame.'

Reluctantly she explained what he had done.

'He *deliberately* told her that you and he... Without saying a word to you...' Ann compressed her mouth. 'Stupid man. He should have known how she'd react.'

'I've told him that he must tell her the truth, but apparently she refused to believe him,' Tania told her.

'Well, yes, she would, but surely James could convince her...?'

Tania was silent for so long that Ann frowned and asked softly, 'What is it? What have I said?'

'Nothing, really. It's just that he doesn't believe Nicholas either. He came round here the other day and virtually threatened to ruin my business if I wouldn't give Nicholas up.'

'He *what*? Oh, I *can't* believe it!'

'Well, it's true,' Tania told her defensively.

Ann looked at her for a moment and then admitted, 'Well, of course, he *has* always been extremely protective of Clarissa. There was a lot of gossip when their parents died; whispers that Clarissa had had a complete breakdown. She's that type, of course, and I suppose if it's true James would want to protect her from any kind of emotional anxiety, but, really, the remedy lies in her own hands. Much as I deplore Nicholas's methods, there's no doubt she hasn't treated the poor man very well.'

'No,' Tania agreed shortly. 'But I can't help wishing that he'd found someone else to use as his supposed "lover". I'm worried, Ann,' she admitted huskily, surprised to hear herself saying the words, when she had always been so cautious about confiding in others, so proud of her independence, so determined to rely only on herself.

It was a measure of how much James had unnerved and frightened her that she should feel this need to confide in Ann and seek her advice, her wise counsel.

'This shop is such a new venture, and if it fails...'

'Fails? It *won't* fail,' Ann told her robustly. 'And if you're worried about the scene Clarissa created, don't be. No one will pay the slightest attention to her. She isn't very popular locally, you know. Not like James.'

'No,' Tania agreed hollowly. 'But it isn't Clarissa who worries me.'

Ann frowned at her.

'You *don't* mean you took James's threat seriously? Oh, Tania, I'm sure he didn't mean it. He's not that sort of man. I expect he was just feeling worried and anxious about Clarissa. She probably wound him up to come down here and warn you off. Believe me, he's one of the kindest, most genuine men. When we were going through a rather difficult patch, he commissioned Tom to virtually redecorate his home from top to bottom. That commission saved our lives.'

'He doesn't like me,' Tania told her stiffly, fiddling with an empty box and refusing to look directly at Ann. 'I expect he considers me an outsider... a trouble-maker.'

Ann looked unhappily at her.

'No, I'm sure you're wrong. Once Nicholas has talked to him...'

'It hasn't made any difference. He *still* believes that Nicholas is my lover.' She took a shaky breath and disclosed flatly, 'He even made a snide remark about Lucy, about her birth and the fact that I wasn't married. I was eighteen when she was born,' she told Ann fiercely. 'Eighteen, that's all.'

To her chagrin, she discovered that her throat was clogged with tears.

'Don't let it upset you,' Ann comforted her. 'I'm sure he didn't mean it, and as for him threatening you . . . I'm sure he just spoke in the heat of the moment——'

She broke off as a customer walked into the shop, quickly followed by two more, glancing at her watch and saying she must leave.

Thanking her for her support, Tania turned to serve the newcomers.

Ann might think that James Warren was the best thing since sliced bread, but she didn't share her view. Without him to support her, she suspected that Clarissa would very quickly have accepted Nicholas's admission that they were not lovers.

Stop thinking about it, she chided herself firmly. You've got work to do.

CHAPTER FIVE

TANIA certainly had plenty to keep her busy, and it was six o'clock before she finally managed to close the door behind her last customer.

Wearily picking up the discarded stock and returning it to its boxes, she decided that she'd better go round to the Fieldings' and collect Lucy before she fell asleep standing up.

She had never felt so tired in her life, but it was a grateful exhaustion that came from the realisation that her sales for the day were going to far exceed her expectations.

She could not hope for business to continue like this, of course, but it was a good start, and with another week to go before all the children were finally back at school she could at least hope for a certain amount of continuing sales.

Once they *were* back at school there would be a lull, of course, but hopefully only a short one, with Christmas not so very far away.

She thought of all the bright, shiny wellingtons she had ordered, the snow boots and waterproofs, the pretty dancing shoes and the sturdy outdoor wear, and as she locked the shop door and hurried down towards the Fieldings' shop she found she was mentally planning her pre-Christmas window display.

On the way home she tried to concentrate on Lucy's bright chatter but discovered that her thoughts were returning time and time again to the altercation in the shop and the cold, biting look James had given her.

Ridiculous to feel so apprehensive. *What*, after all, could he do? Publicly denounce her as a husband-stealer? Who in this day and age would care? All that would achieve would be to give rise to a good deal of speculation and gossip of a type which would surely be as painful and unwelcome to Clarissa as it would be to her.

So what else *could* he do? Damage her business? She shivered, and hugged her jacket more firmly around her. She must tell Nicholas that he had to find a way of convincing not only Clarissa but James as well that he had lied, but *would* he do so? He had promised her once already that he would put things right but so far...

Because she had known that she would have to spend most of the evening engaged in doing her accounts, she had hired a video of one of Lucy's favourite films, and as soon as supper was over Ann brought Susan round to share the treat, firmly announcing that she wasn't stopping since she knew that Tania had work to do.

'If you're still worrying about James, don't,' she advised Tania before she left. 'He'll soon come to realise that you aren't the type to become involved with someone else's man. In fact I don't think I've ever met a woman who is so scrupulously uninterested in the male sex,' she added thoughtfully. 'I'm not trying to pry, Tania, but if you could perhaps approach James yourself and explain...'

'No,' Tania told her fiercely. 'It's no good. He wouldn't believe me. Anyway, I don't even know where he lives or——'

'That's easy. He has a beautiful house just outside town. It overlooks the river, and it's one of the most serene houses I've ever seen. You'll probably have passed it.'

When she described where it was, Tania realised that it was the house she had seen on their walk. She had envied its owners then without knowing their identity. It seemed so unfair, she reflected acidly now, that when both Clarissa and James had so much they should not be content, more than content. Clarissa on her own she could probably have handled, but James... He intimidated her, she recognised, but not exactly on a personal level. She still couldn't entirely banish that traitorous knowledge that she had looked at him, if only for a second, and wondered about him as a man, but she *was* afraid of his power; of his ability to destroy her business and with it the new life she wanted so much for Lucy. It seemed so unfair, so...so stupid. He was apparently an intelligent man. Surely he could see that Nicholas adored Clarissa?

'It was only a thought,' Ann told her gently. 'I'll come back for Susie about nine, if that's OK with you?'

By nine o'clock, her body tense with concentration, Tania knew that financially the day had been an outstanding success. She would need to reorder certain very popular lines and it would be several weeks before she was able to assess which lines she needed to carry on a permanent basis and which could be discarded, but she was pleased to be able to cautiously note that her own instincts on which shoes would most appeal to her customers had been proved right.

An hour later, having said goodbye to Ann and put Lucy to bed, she acknowledged that she could do with an early night herself. Physically she was exhausted, but mentally...

Mentally she was far too unpleasantly alert, as she discovered once she was actually in bed, but it wasn't a happy alertness. Over and over again, her thoughts kept returning to Clarissa Forbes... and not just to Clarissa but to James as well.

Nicholas had no right, no right at all to involve her in his marital problems, and added to her irritation against him was a growing sense of injustice, of having been used without any thought being given to the possible consequences of his actions.

She was, she discovered, fast going from a lukewarm liking of him to a growing feeling that he was essentially a rather weak character, who had probably contributed as much to his own marital problems as had his wife.

He claimed that Clarissa always put her brother first, that he as her husband was always pushed into second place, but Clarissa obviously loved him. Otherwise, why should she be so determined to hang on to him? The pair of them wanted their heads banging together, she thought tiredly as she tried to court sleep. Thank goodness tomorrow was Sunday and she could have a relaxing day.

She was drifting off to sleep when she heard the sharp, splintering sound of breaking glass, followed by the shrill wail of her newly installed alarm. Immediately she was out of bed, rushing over to the window, just in time to see someone running away.

Too angry to think of caution, she pulled on her dressing-gown and ran downstairs, unlocking the door through into the shop area and switching on the lights.

The front of the shop was covered in shards of glass; the alarm was still wailing frantically, and she could see a gaping hole right in the front of her window, where not only was the glass smashed but the actual frame had been damaged as well.

Shock had now caught hold of her, and she stood dizzily staring at the window, pushing one hand into her hair as she tried to get her brain to work. The sound of the alarm was jangling her already overstretched nerves, destroying her ability to think logically.

The alarm was connected directly with the police station. Did that mean that they would come out or ought she to telephone? And what if the noise of the alarm woke Lucy and frightened her? She ought to go upstairs and check but, if she left the shop, might not whoever had broken the window come back? The sound of the alarm had obviously frightened them off. She had no idea yet if any stock was actually missing from the window, but she remembered nervously that her takings for the day were upstairs in her living-room, albeit locked away in a secure cash-box, but even so... In future she would make sure she banked every day's takings in her local bank's night safe. She dreaded to think what might have happened if she hadn't had that alarm...if the thieves had broken in upstairs...

She was shivering, she discovered, trembling with reaction and weakness.

She heard a car driving down the road and instinctively tensed, only to relax as she recognised the familiar colour and insignia of a police patrol car.

As the driver got out, frowning as he surveyed the damage, she stepped forward automatically, but he saw her and waved her back.

'You haven't got any shoes on,' he reminded her through the broken window, 'and the floor's covered in glass. Is there another way I can come in?'

Shakily Tania directed him to the back door and went to open it for him.

'What happened?' he asked her once he was inside.

Briefly she told him how she had been woken up by the sound of breaking glass and had only managed to see someone running away.

'It was probably just vandals,' she commented, sighing a little as she remembered the iron grilles that had been such a familiar feature of the small parade of shops near her old flat. She had come here to escape from that kind of thing. To live more freely, more safely, more healthily.

'Mm... could be, although it isn't the kind of thing we normally get happening round here. Pub brawls, teenage scuffles now and again, the odd bit of trouble here and there... but smashing shop windows... Just as well you'd got that alarm.'

'Yes. My insurance company insisted on it. As you say, just as well.'

'Mm... Well, you won't have had time to see if anything's missing yet... Only just opened, haven't you?'

'Yes.' Tania told him. She was beginning to feel extraordinarily light-headed and rather peculiar.

'Yes. The wife said she was going to call in and see if she could get our two fixed up with something they couldn't destroy in under two months.' He gave a faint sigh. 'Boots are what you play football in, she tells them, but do they pay any attention? Kids! They think money grows on trees. You feeling OK?' he asked her, frowning as he noticed her growing pallor. 'Bit of a shock, something like this. Is your husband...?'

'I... I'm not married,' Tania told him quickly. 'I... would it be all right if I went upstairs to check on my little girl? If she's woken up she might be feeling frightened.'

'Yes, you go ahead. We can't do much down here, other than make the window secure. You'll want your insurance people to see it. Is there anyone local who could come over and spend the rest of the night with you?'

Tania looked alarmed and he assured her, 'I doubt that whoever did it will come back, but you're bound to feel a bit apprehensive. Could ask for a WPC to come along for a while, but we're short-staffed and on a Saturday night...'

'It's kind of you,' Tania said quickly. 'But I'll be fine.'

She had switched off the alarm when she went to let him in the back door, and now, in his solid, reassuring presence, she was beginning to feel her shock easing slightly.

When she went upstairs she discovered that Lucy was fast asleep. She offered the policeman a cup of tea and then with his help checked the window and discovered that nothing was actually missing.

'Made a mess of it though, haven't they?' he mused as he helped her. 'Pity, because a nice shop window always attracts customers, and I doubt you'll have this one back to rights for a couple of weeks.'

It was a point that had not yet occurred to Tania, but she recognised that he was right. Who would be tempted to buy children's shoes from a shop with its window boarded up while it awaited repair? She went cold as she remembered how busy the shop-front fitters had been and how long she had had to wait for the original window to be fitted. This break-in, although it hadn't resulted in the loss of any stock, could seriously affect her sales.

Numbly she recollected James Warren's threat. It hadn't been him she had seen running away, of course, but could it be possible that he was behind this attack on her shop, on her business, on her security? She shivered and the policeman gave her a concerned look.

'You sure you're all right?'

'I'm fine,' she lied. Oh, God, what if this was the start of a campaign of intimidation against her? What if...? Stop it, she warned herself as her thoughts threatened to go wildly out of control. Stop it. Even if he is responsible you're not going to give in...you're not going to let him frighten you. *You* haven't done anything.

It was over an hour before the policeman finally left, having told her that he suspected that they would probably never find the culprit and warning her to lock the doors behind him.

After that, of course, although she went back to bed, it was impossible for her to sleep. It would be Monday before she could get in touch with her insurance broker...before she could do anything at all, really.

When she finally went to sleep she felt as though a huge black cloud had engulfed her whole world. Even in her darkest moments of the past, even when she had known she was pregnant with Lucy...even when she had faced the reality that she and Lucy would always have to face the world on their own, she had not felt as vulnerable and afraid as she did now.

Had James Warren been responsible? What kind of man could do a thing like this? He must have known how much it would terrify her. He must have known. But then why should he show any compassion, any pity for her? He *wanted* to terrify her, he *wanted* to frighten her... He *wanted* to hurt her.

The next morning she felt no better. Ann, who had called after she had seen the broken window on her way to the Post Office to collect her Sunday papers, was full of briskly firm optimism.

Tom, it seemed, knew Tania's insurance broker very well, and would, she was sure, give him a ring and ask him if it was possible for him to come straight round.

'And as for repairing the window, well, I don't think it's as bad as it looks. I'm sure we'll be able to do something. You must have been scared out of your wits when you heard the noise. Who on earth would do such a thing? Nothing like this has ever happened here before.'

Tania almost told her her suspicions, but then she remembered Ann's enthusiastic praise of James Warren and held her tongue. Ann would probably think she was becoming paranoid. She wasn't sure if she wasn't herself. After all, she had no proof that James was involved.

But he *had* threatened her. She shivered, and Ann suggested warmly,

'Look, why don't both of you come back with me? I'll get Tom to give Larry Barnes a ring straight away.'

'Oh, Ann, I always seem to be bringing you my problems. Your family will be sick of the sight of me and Lucy.'

'Nonsense, and besides, what else are friends for?'

If Larry Barnes, her insurance broker, resented having his Sunday peace disturbed, he didn't show it. He was a man in his mid-fifties, with a calm, reassuring manner.

No, she wouldn't have any problems with her insurance claim, he assured Tania, and yes, she could go ahead and get the window repaired just as soon as she liked. In fact, he thought he knew someone who would be able to do the job for her almost immediately, and, of course, he reminded her, there was a loss-of-business clause in her policy which meant that if the lack of a window did affect her sales then she could potentially claim on her policy.

Nevertheless, Tania discovered that the whole incident had left her feeling nervous and on edge.

Late on Sunday evening, when she should have been in bed, she discovered that she was still prowling round her living-room, unable to settle, afraid to go to bed in case there was a recurrence of the previous night's attempted break-in.

Eventually, at one o'clock, she managed to persuade herself that if she didn't at least try to get some sleep she'd be too exhausted to work, but even so her sleep was fitful and disturbed, full of intimidating images and imagined fears, so that she woke up more than once with her heart pounding and her mouth dry with tension.

It was halfway through Monday morning when the men were busy at work refitting the shop window, and she had closeted herself upstairs in her sitting-room to do some paperwork, when someone knocked on her sitting-room door and she opened it to discover Nicholas standing outside.

'I heard this morning about the attempted break-in,' he told her. 'What happened? Are you OK?'

'I'm fine,' Tania assured him, noting how strained and drawn he looked, and, as she offered him a cup of coffee, she wondered if he, like her, suspected that James might have been behind the attack on her shop.

Lucy, who had been playing in her room, came through into the sitting room when she heard Nicholas's voice. She gave him a shy smile, responding with cautious friendliness to his questions.

Tania explained that it would be a couple of days yet before Lucy started at her new school.

'I didn't just come round because of the break-in,' Nicholas told her in a low voice when she handed him his mug of coffee.

'Alec let slip about the scene that Clarissa created here on Saturday. I wanted to apologise to you.'

Her consciousness of Lucy's presence in the room with them, even though she appeared to be engrossed in the book she was reading, restrained Tania from being as frank with him as she would have liked. Instead she had to content herself with saying meaningfully, 'I'm sure that once she realises and accepts the truth it won't happen again.'

Nicholas shrugged his shoulders and said defeatedly, 'She won't even listen to me any more. She keeps on threatening to leave me and take the boys. She creates these terrible scenes, and simply won't listen to anything I have to say. She's always been highly strung. I've tried suggesting to her that she ought to see a doctor. She had a breakdown when her mother was killed, and I'm very much afraid . . .'

Tania frowned. Could it be that there was rather more to Clarissa's behaviour than simply the self-ishness of a spoilt child-woman who was used to having her every whim indulged?

'Have you spoken to James about this?' she asked Nicholas in some concern. Privately she considered that if Clarissa was suffering from some kind of emotional maladjustment, as she might well be, then Nicholas's trying to deal with it by pretending to be having an affair with another woman was hardly a sensible thing to do, but then it was her belief that the male sex rarely understood the female, and men were notoriously reluctant to deal with any problems that involved emotions, either their own or someone else's.

'Oh, he always sides with Clarissa, no matter what I say,' Nicholas told her moodily. 'He'd probably just think I was trying to put her down, and, of course, she's always as sweet as sugar when James is there.'

Tania made a wry face. Sweet as sugar wasn't exactly how she would have described Clarissa's behaviour on Saturday.

'But, Nicholas,' she pressed, 'have you considered that she might be quite seriously ill, and if she's already suffered one breakdown...'

'I've tried to tell her as much but every time I raise the subject she flies off the handle and accuses me of trying to get rid of her, of wanting to have her locked up in a mental asylum. The whole situation is getting completely out of control. I just do not know where to turn any more. I'm even beginning to wonder if it's me... If *I'm* the one causing her problems, if she wouldn't be better off without me.'

Tania's frown deepened. She was beginning to recognise that Nicholas, while essentially a pleasant enough man, was, in his own way, perhaps just as spoiled as his wife. Like a small child, he was perhaps punishing *her* because she was not giving him the amount of love and attention he felt she should. Both of them should perhaps have married far stronger characters, people who were capable of coping with their insecurities and vulnerability, people with the strength to cosset and carry them. She could never, for instance, imagine a man like James Warren reacting to Clarissa's apparent unreasonableness in the way that Nicholas was doing. Perhaps after all it was no wonder that Clarissa turned so often from her husband to her stepbrother.

'You have two children,' she pointed out softly to Nicholas now. 'And they need you, both of you. If you can't persuade Clarissa to see a doctor yourself, Nicholas, then I really think you should try to takes James into your confidence. And while you're at it will you please tell him that you and I are not having an affair?' she added in a low voice.

Lucy, who was sitting on the window-seat with her book, suddenly raised her head and announced, 'Mum, there's a huge car parked outside, and the man's coming into the shop.'

Tania went over to the window to look outside. Nicholas joined her.

'Hell,' he swore under his breath. 'That's James's car. What on earth is he doing here?'

As she stared at the immaculate dark blue Jaguar without really seeing it, Tania felt her stomach muscles clenching in a fierce protest.

Had he come to see just how she was reacting to his threats? To admit that he was responsible for the damage to her shop? Or perhaps even to issue further threats, to harass and terrorise her even further? It would have served him right if she had told the police about him, she reflected bitterly. But then they were hardly likely to have believed her. Why on earth would such an important and well thought of local businessman arrange for someone to smash the shop window of someone as insignificant as herself? No... It wouldn't have done the slightest good.

Even so.

'I'd better go down and see what he wants,' she began, only to stop when they heard the imperious rap on her sitting-room door.

When she opened it the look he gave her made her blood run cold. The eye contact between them was antagonistic and bitter, and Tania hated the way he made her look away first, her face flooding with colour as he stepped past her and said with cold evenness, 'Nicholas, I thought I saw your car outside. Thinking of leaving us, Ms Carter?' he asked her with an effrontery that strangled her protests before she could utter them. 'A wise decision. Presumably Nicholas is here in his capacity as your legal adviser?'

Nicholas frowned at his brother-in-law.

'I'm not here in any business capacity, James. I'd heard about the break-in and naturally I called to see if Tania was OK.'

'Naturally?' The dark eyebrows rose, the hard mouth twisting contemptuously as James Warren looked from Nicholas's stubborn face to Tania's flushed, angry one. 'Very thoughtful of you, I'm sure, but, since you must by now have reassured yourself that Ms Carter hasn't suffered any after-effects from what was after all little more than an excess of youthful high spirits, perhaps you might care to remember that you promised to take Clarissa and the boys into Chester for lunch.'

'Oh, my God! Yes... I'd forgotten. I'll have to go, I'm afraid, Tania.'

He reached for her hand, but instead of shaking it as Tania had expected, he cupped it in both of his in a far more intimate gesture than she had expected.

Impossible to stop herself from glancing sideways to see how James was reacting to his brother-in-law's intimate tenderness. The hard, dangerous look he gave her made her tremble. She fought against the cowardly impulse to open her mouth and tell him that he was wrong, that it wasn't what he thought... that it wasn't even what she wanted, but stubbornness and pride held her silent, making her give Nicholas a far more tender smile than she would otherwise have done.

Anxious not to be left alone with James so that he could repeat his threats or insult her still further, she determinedly walked downstairs with Nicholas, so that James was left with no alternative but to accompany them. In the noisy shop, ringing with the sound of the men repairing the window, she said firmly, 'It was kind of you to call, Nicholas. I hope you enjoy your lunch,' and then immediately turned to James and said coldly, 'Now that you've got what you came for, Mr Warren, I'm sure there's no reason for you to stay.'

She could tell that he was angry with her from the dark glitter in his eyes, and, as Nicholas turned away from her, he stood in front of her so that Nicholas couldn't see his expression or overhear what he was saying and told her icily, 'You may think you're being very clever, but try thinking about this. It isn't just my sister you're hurting. You know that she and Nicholas have two children, who need them both.'

She was angry enough to be reckless, temper running through her veins like Greek fire as she snapped back.

'Oh, really? Well, according to local gossip, they're hardly likely to miss their father, not when they have such a devoted and caring uncle to turn to! No one dictates to me how I run my life. No one!'

She might have gone on to tell him what she thought of his cruel plans to ruin her business and frighten her away from the area, but Nicholas had turned round and was watching them both, patently waiting for James to join him.

Halfway back up the stairs she had to rest because her legs were shaking so much.

This had got to stop. Somehow she had to find a way of ensuring that Nicholas not only told his brother-in-law the truth, but also made sure that he accepted it.

It was no use her saying anything, nor prompting Nicholas in James's presence. It was patently obvious that he wouldn't believe her.

But she could not go on like this for much longer. Her nerves were already overstrained as it was!

CHAPTER SIX

DESPITE her fears that the broken shop window would put off potential customers, Tania discovered that news of the attempted break-in prompted an increase in business through people calling in both out of curiosity and in genuine concern, and by the time the window was replaced later in the week she was able to confide to Ann, who had phoned her for a chat, that her first few days of business had proved so busy that she had had to ring some of her suppliers to request urgent replacement stock.

'And this is only the start,' Ann promised her. 'You wait and see. It's my belief that people are gradually turning away from the kind of shopping which involves all the stress involved in dragging their kids around huge soulless shopping centres. It's all part of the nostalgia for the past and the need to return to a more natural way of life. We find we're getting more and more customers who say they can't stand another fraught trip round some vast superstore where they can't find what they want and when they do paying for it involves an exasperating wait at a supermarket-style checkout.

'Which reminds me, I wanted to ask you if you'd put away a couple of pairs of those American-style baseball boots for the boys. I want to put them in their Christmas stockings. Susan has informed me that she wants to learn tap-dancing, if you please, so it will have to be tap shoes for her.

'The police haven't been back to you to say if they've found out who broke your window?'

'No,' Tania told her. 'I don't think they will be, either.'

'Well, I doubt that it will happen again. Not now that the perpetrator realises how well you're alarmed,' Ann told her comfortingly.

Tania said nothing. She wasn't sure that the presence of any alarm system, no matter how sophisticated, would deter the person she believed was really responsible. Neither had the object of the exercise been to steal from her. At least not in a material sense. To steal away her peace of mind, her security, and perhaps ultimately even her self-respect, yes; she could believe James Warren to be guilty of those crimes.

She shivered a little as she replaced the telephone receiver.

Soon it would be time for Tania and Ann to fetch Lucy home from school. It seemed so unfair to Tania that through no fault of her own she should be suffering this heavy burden of apprehension and dread, especially when Lucy had settled down so well to their new life.

She was full of bright chatter about her new school. Tania had no wish to push her daughter into academic success but there was no doubt that a good education, good qualifications were essential these days if one wanted a well-paid career. From her own experience she knew how important it was that a woman could support herself financially. She had no wish for Lucy to fall into the dangerous trap of becoming dependent on a man or a relationship to the detriment of her own self-worth and independence.

If her business continued in its present fashion, she would have to seriously consider taking on part-time staff, and maybe not merely a girl to help on Saturdays, but someone whom she could leave in charge of the shop occasionally during the week, so that she could attend the various trade fairs and do her buying.

She had just finished serving a pleasant girl with a toddler just ready for her first pair of proper shoes when the shop bell rang again.

She looked up with a smile that faded to sharp apprehension as she saw Clarissa Forbes walking into the shop. This time she was alone and a brief glance outside assured Tania that her intimidating stepbrother was thankfully nowhere in sight.

'Clarissa,' Tania welcomed her, firmly determined not to give her any reason to reinforce her idiotic belief that Tania was having an affair with her husband.

However, the moment she spoke to her, Clarissa went white with fury and spat viciously at Tania, 'Oh, yes, you go ahead and smile, but you won't be smiling for much longer. If you *think* I'm simply going to stand aside and let you walk off with my husband, you'll soon discover that you're wrong. Nicholas is mine and I don't intend to give him up to you or anyone else.'

Tania stared at her, quickly taking in her dilated eyes and aggressive pose. Tension emanated from her too-thin body, and her facial muscles were rigid with the intensity of her emotions.

'Clarissa, please calm down. You've got it all wrong. Nicholas and I are *not* having an affair.'

'Don't lie to me. That's what Nicky tried to do, but I know the truth. You both might pretend that it's over between you, but I know it isn't. When did it start? When you first came here, or was it before that? Did he meet you before you even moved here? Did the two of you plan the whole thing? That you would move here?

'Well, if you think that I'm just going to stand by and let you walk off with my husband, you'll soon discover just how wrong you are.'

Recognising the growing signs of impending hysteria, Tania attempted to calm her down, frightened now not on her own account so much as on Clarissa's. The other woman was plainly under an intense emotional strain, and as she tried to interrupt her Tania felt a flash of fierce irritation and anger against both Nicholas and James. Surely one of them must have the wit to see that Clarissa wasn't entirely well?

'Clarissa, please, you've got all this wrong. Talk to Nicholas. Let him explain to you, I promise you that I am not and never have had an affair with him. Look, why don't I ring Nicholas now and——?'

'No! I don't want him here, but you do, don't you? You want him to send me away so that you can be alone with him. Well, I'm not going to let you destroy my marriage, and if you don't give him up I'll make you sorry you were ever born,' she threatened dramatically before turning on her heel and storming out of the shop before Tania could restrain her.

After she had gone Tania stared at the phone, gnawing indecisively at her bottom lip, wondering whether she ought to ring Nicholas and warn him what had happened. But then might not Clarissa take that as further proof that they *were* having an affair should she find out about it?

Her own inner sense of responsibility made her feel that there must be something she could do to help the other woman who so plainly did need some kind of help. Tania had gone beyond feeling irritated resentment towards her now. That anger and resentment had given way to concern.

'Something on your mind?' Ann asked her later when they were walking the girls back from school.

Briefly Tania explained what had happened.

'Mm... And you think she's suffering from some kind of depression or something?'

'Well, it could be, or it could be something deeper, something perhaps associated with the death of her mother and James's father. She's obviously emotionally very highly strung. In some ways it's almost as though she *wants* to believe that Nicholas and I are having an affair.'

'Mm. She probably realises she's over-reacting, and in some way insisting on believing Nick is being unfaithful to her gives her a logical justification for her behaviour. I'm surprised James hasn't realised what's happening, but then he's been away such a lot this year. The electronics company he owns does a lot of business with the States and he's been over there for months at a time setting up some new deal or other.

'I heard on the grapevine the other day that his new contract with the Americans has been signed now, and that he should be home far more often in future. Maybe he'll realise what's going on...'

'I doubt it,' Tania told her grittily. 'Like his stepsister, he seems determined to blame me.'

'It's really unlike him to react like that. Perhaps he secretly fancies you himself,' Ann teased her, 'and he's jealous of Nick's supposed involvement with you.'

Tania forced herself to laugh, but inside she was desperately aware of the unwanted twist of sensation Ann's light-hearted comment had brought.

Oh, God, she thought shakily as she and Ann parted company, please don't let that happen... Why, after all these years of being completely indifferent to the male sex, should she go and find herself so dangerously aware of the one man who was most unlikely to reciprocate the fiercely pagan emotions seizing her? Was it because she *knew* that there could be no question of him sharing her desire that she had allowed these feelings to spring up inside her? Because she *knew* there was no possibility, no danger of her ever becoming either emotionally or physically involved with him, because in some perverse way it was safe for her to desire him, rather in the same way that a teenager desired a pop star? They were thoughts she did not wish to pursue.

*   *   *

Tomorrow would be her second Saturday with the shop. She couldn't expect business to be as brisk as it had been last week, but nevertheless it was with a mingled feeling of anxiety and elation that she got up the following morning.

She had arranged that Ann's niece, Peggy, would come in for a couple of hours at lunchtime to give her a break, and Ann had very generously insisted that Lucy spend the morning and the afternoon with them, responding cheerfully when Tania had protested that she was imposing far too much on her kindness.

'Nonsense, there'll come a time when you'll be able to do something similar for me.'

'Well, I hope so. But please send Lucy home at lunchtime. She's had more than enough free meals with you...'

'I will,' Ann promised her. 'Twelve o'clock sharp she shall be despatched home.'

'I'll come and meet her. I know it's only a few doors away, but even so.'

At five to twelve, just as Tania was about to put on her jacket and hand over to Peggy, a customer walked into the shop accompanied by a pair of twins and two older children, all of them boys.

When she announced that she needed shoes for all of them, Tania felt that it would be unfair to expect Peggy to deal with them, and, removing her jacket, said smilingly that she would do what she could to help.

In the end it was almost a quarter to one before all four children were satisfactorily shod.

'It's wonderful to find a shop like this one,' their mother told Tania. 'Normally buying anything for them is an absolute nightmare. My husband absolutely refuses to come with me, and the kids generally end up squabbling.'

Smiling her sympathy, Tania walked with them to the door.

Once they had gone she turned to Peggy and told her, 'Things should quieten down a little now while everyone goes home for lunch. I'll just pop upstairs and see what Lucy's up to. She must be starving, poor child.'

But when she opened the door into the flat, the living-room was empty, the whole flat oddly silent.

She called Lucy's name and opened her bedroom door, frowning at its emptiness.

Had Ann forgotten that she had promised to send Lucy home at twelve? Perhaps if the girls had become involved in a game... But the Fieldings normally sat down for lunch at twelve-thirty on the dot... and it was now almost one.

An indefinable maternal apprehension gripped hold of her. Without stopping to collect her jacket, she hurried downstairs and outside and then down the narrow passage which separated their building from its neighbour and out into the street, looking anxiously up and down it, in search of the familiar russet-haired figure of her small daughter.

Only there was no sign of Lucy.

Frantically anxious now, she hurried down the street, and into the Fieldings' shop.

Tom Fielding was drinking a mug of tea, which he put down when he saw the anxiety in her face, asking quickly, 'Tania, what's wrong? Not another break-in?'

'No, no, it's not that... It's Lucy... She hasn't come home yet, and I was wondering...'

Tom stood up, his own face now shadowed and concerned.

'But she left here at five to twelve. That's——'

'Over an hour ago,' Tania finished shakily for him. 'You don't suppose...? She couldn't have come back, perhaps?'

'Well, she could have done, I suppose. Look, you go up and have a word with Ann.'

Anxiously Tania hurried upstairs, knocking tensely on the Fieldings' sitting-room door.

Ann opened it, her smile fading to concern as Tania asked her if Lucy was with her.

'No, she isn't. I sent her home at five to twelve as we arranged.'

'Oh, my God. I meant to meet her and walk back with her, but this woman came into the shop with four boys, and I couldn't leave poor Peggy to deal with them. I thought Lucy must have come back and gone upstairs, but there's no sign of her in the flat.'

She was beginning to shake with fear.

Ann took hold of her and said firmly, 'Now, don't panic. Are you sure she's not at home? She couldn't be in her bedroom, perhaps?'

'No... No, I checked.'

'Well, perhaps she met someone... a schoolfriend...'

'No,' Tania shook her head and said stiffly. 'She would never go off with anyone else. She knows.

I've always taught her. She's been brought up in a city, Ann. She knows all about the dangers of speaking to strangers...of——'

Her voice broke and Ann hugged her tightly.

'We'll find her, don't you worry. Let me go and ring the police.'

'The police.' Her eyes dark with fear for her daughter, Tania stared mutely at her friend.

'It's the only sensible thing to do,' Ann told her gently. 'She's probably perfectly safe.'

Tania started to tremble violently, her mind forcing her to dwell on all that Ann was not saying.

It was every parent's nightmare that her child should disappear. It happened so often, so tragically... Sickness clawed at her stomach.

'No...not Lucy,' she whispered chokily. 'Oh, please, God, don't let anything have happened to her!'

'Come on...you won't help her by breaking down,' Ann warned her firmly. 'Look, you sit down for a moment while I ring the police.'

Half an hour later, while her mind ran in frantic circles of fear, anguish and guilt, Tania was trying to answer the questions of the WPC and the detective who had come to the Fieldings' home to interview her.

When they asked her what clothes Lucy was wearing, she had had such a heartbreakingly real image of her small daughter when she had said goodbye to her that morning that she had had to fight not to break down completely.

'Don't worry,' they told her. 'She's probably gone off somewhere with a friend and totally lost track of time.'

Tania refused to accept any comfort. Lucy wouldn't do that. And besides, her closest friend was Susan. Susan who had nervously told the WPC that Lucy had told her she was coming straight back after lunch.

'Is there anyone who might have taken her away? Someone that you know,' the WPC pressed gently. 'Lucy's father...grandparents ...an ex-boyfriend?'

Numbly Tania shook her head. No, there was no one like that... No one.

'Well, try not to worry. We've got people out searching for her. If she's new to the town, it isn't inconceivable that she's even got lost. Does she know anywhere locally, anywhere where she might have wanted to go?'

'We walked along by the river one day. We saw an otter, and a dog... Lucy loves dogs,' she told them numbly. 'I'd half promised her that in the spring...'

She started to shake, unable to stop herself from thinking that when the spring came she might well be alone...that Lucy, her precious, vulnerable child...

'I have to ask you this, Tania. It isn't a criticism. We all lose our tempers at times, but had you and Lucy had a quarrel? Could she perhaps have felt reluctant to come home?'

Tania shook her head.

'No. We didn't have that sort of relationship. She isn't a naughty child.'

'I can confirm that,' Ann put in quietly. 'And when she left here she seemed perfectly happy. She told us that you'd promised her fresh salmon for lunch.'

'Yes, I had,' Tania agreed jerkily. 'It's her favourite. An extravagance but far better for her than fish fingers . . . and I want her to grow up healthily. Girls these days come under so much pressure from the media. I don't want her to grow up feeling that she has to conform to some advertisers' ideal of what a woman should be.'

Her voice started to shake and she covered her face with her hands as the tears started to flow.

Oh, God, she was so frightened. . .not for herself but for Lucy, her precious little Lucy.

'It will be all right,' the WPC told her, but Tania wasn't convinced. When the police suggested that it might be as well if she went home just in case Lucy found her own way back there, Tania got numbly to her feet.

'Don't worry about the shop,' Ann told her. 'I'll go down and take over from Peggy.'

The rest of the afternoon passed in a blur of growing tension and anxiety. Someone stayed with her all the time, but slowly her hopes that Lucy might after all simply have got lost or distracted faded into an agonised certainty that something unbelievably dreadful had happened to her daughter.

And then at five o'clock the WPC who had stayed with her and who was standing by the living-room window frowned and asked her urgently, 'Come here, will you, Tania?'

Awkwardly she went to join her, her heart literally leaping into her throat as she looked out into the street and saw Lucy getting out of the back of James Warren's dark blue Jaguar.

'Is that your daughter?' the WPC asked her.

It was impossible for her to speak. She could only nod her head whilst tears of relief poured down her face.

Through them she saw Lucy confidently slip her hand into James's as they walked towards the door, then James stopped and looked up at her.

The expression on his face made her heart twist a second time. She had never seen in another adult face such a combination of sorrow, anguish and guilt. It was a look that so closely mimicked her own emotions that she found she was holding her breath, hardly daring to breathe, hardly daring to do anything other than simply stand there as Lucy came hurtling up the stairs and burst into the room saying excitedly.

'Mum, you'll never guess what, James has promised me that he'll buy me a dog for my birthday, if you say it's all right ... and he's going to teach me how to train it properly so that it won't be like Rupert. Not a spaniel, though, they're too scatty, and besides they're gun dogs really and they need lots and lots of exercise.'

While she paused to draw breath, the WPC walked slowly towards them and said quietly, 'Hello, Lucy. Have you had a nice afternoon?'

Lucy beamed her affirmation, and the woman said quietly over her head to Tania, 'I'll report in and let them know she's back safely.' She then turned to James and said quietly, 'I'm afraid I'm going to have to ask you to wait here for a few minutes, sir. Lucy has been missing all afternoon without her mother's knowledge.'

'I can explain everything,' James answered emotionlessly.

He suddenly looked so tired, so defeated, so drained that Tania actually discovered she felt compassion for him.

Initially, when she had seen Lucy getting out of his car, she had been overwhelmed by a shock of realisation that when she had told the police she knew of no one who might want to kidnap her child she had been wrong. But when James had threatened her she had never dreamed he might try to hurt her through Lucy.

And then she had seen the look on his face and she had known instinctively that whatever had happened to Lucy, that whoever had been responsible for her disappearance, it was not this man.

'I think it might be as well if I went back to the station with you,' he told the policewoman, and then turned to Tania and added quietly, 'Will it be all right if I leave my car outside? I need to talk with you anyway. I could call back later if you'll let me.'

Numbly she nodded her head. 'Thank you.'

The words were emotionless like every other word he had uttered and yet Tania was intensely aware that beneath his calm manner there was bitter anguish.

'If you'd like to come this way, sir.'

If the policewoman was aware of who he was, she wasn't allowing it to influence her.

Once she was alone with Lucy and she had assured herself that her child was physically and emotionally safe, she asked as casually as she could, 'How did you come to meet James, poppet? I was worried about you, you know, when you didn't come home for lunch...'

'That's what I told the lady,' Lucy assured her gravely. 'I said you would be worried, but she said that it was all right and that I was to go home with her. She said that you were busy with Uncle Nicholas,' Lucy added innocently.

It was as though a huge fist had closed on her heart, Tania realised.

'This...this lady. Was she...was she Uncle Nicholas's wife?'

'Yes,' Lucy told her nodding vigorously. 'They've got a really big house, Mum, and Rupert was there. She let me play with him and she gave me some chocolate biscuits. She kept asking me lots of questions about you and Uncle Nicholas and then she started to cry. She frightened me a bit,' Lucy told her innocently, frowning. 'I didn't like it when she cried.'

'Did she... Did she...say anything else to you?' Tania asked her. She had no wish to frighten Lucy, or to make her realise just how much danger she might have been in. It was plain now that Clarissa was far more disturbed than Tania had realised.

'No, not really. I didn't really want to go with her, but she got hold of my arm, and it hurt, and then she pushed me into her car and I was too frightened to get out,' Lucy added. 'But it was fine playing with Rupert.

'And then James came in, and she started to cry some more. He said that he was going to bring me home. They talked lots and lots and she grabbed hold of his arm and begged him not to leave her. I didn't like it then, and I don't think James did either.'

'No. I'm sure he didn't,' Tania agreed slowly, shivering a little.

The phone rang and she picked up the receiver. It was Ann.

'Any news?'

'Yes, Lucy's safely home. James Warren brought her back.'

'James Warren—but——?'

'I can't really talk about it now,' Tania interrupted her, 'but it seems that Clarissa persuaded Lucy to go home with her.'

She heard Ann's shocked gasp and then her friend said tensely, 'The woman must be deranged. What on earth did she think she was doing?'

'I'm not sure and I suspect that she isn't either,' Tania told her tiredly. 'James has gone down to the police station. He said he'd call here afterwards and explain everything to me, but the important thing is that Lucy is safe.'

'Yes,' Ann agreed soberly. 'Look, if you want me to come over and stay the night...'

'No, we'll be fine.'

In truth she would have been glad of Ann's company and she certainly suspected she wouldn't get much sleep, but it didn't do to depend too much on others, and sooner or later she was going to have to confront the fears which had gripped her all afternoon. The important thing was that Lucy was safe. That none of the appalling fates which had tormented Tania had actually overtaken her . . . that while she had no doubt been a little frightened she had probably never been in any physical danger. Certainly it didn't seem as though Clarissa had made any threats against her. From what Lucy had told her it seemed as though Clarissa had been more intent on finding out how much time Nicholas had spent with Tania and her daughter.

And the blame wasn't entirely Clarissa's . . . not entirely. They were all of them in part to blame, all of them. Tania herself might not have been having an affair with Nicholas, but she had been too proud, too stubborn to make sure that Clarissa knew she wasn't. She had additionally recognised that the other woman wasn't well, but she had done nothing to warn someone who might have been able to do something. And why? Because that someone was James. And because of that she had potentially put her child's safety at risk. Through pride and stubbornness and a fear of her own that she was not as indifferent to him as she wanted to be.

Thankfully Lucy had emerged from her ordeal unharmed, but things could have been so different. If Clarissa had decided to punish Lucy for her mother's imagined sins . . . if she had decided . . . Tania started to shudder.

Stop it, she told herself silently. For Lucy's sake she must not give way to her emotions. She must remain calm and in control, outwardly at least.

Inwardly... well, that was a different thing altogether. Inwardly...

All she could do was thank God and James that
her daughter had been safely restored to her.

CHAPTER SEVEN

It was ten o'clock before James returned. Lucy had been in bed for an hour and was fast asleep.

When Tania went downstairs to let him in, the street lighting highlighted his haggard, drawn expression.

'I'm sorry I've been so long, but there were certain formalities. I had to wait for Nicholas to get back from returning the boys to school so that he could sign the consent forms for Clarissa to be admitted to a private hospital, where hopefully...'

He stopped and Tania suggested awkwardly, 'You look exhausted. I was going to have some supper. Would you...?'

'No...nothing to eat, thanks, but a cup of coffee...'

'Yes, of course. Come upstairs. We can talk up there. Lucy is asleep, no doubt dreaming of this puppy you've promised her,' she added wryly.

'I'm sorry. I should have asked you first...but after she'd witnessed Clarissa's hysterics, it was the only thing I could think of to distract her. Poor kid, she must have been terrified, but she hid it well.'

'I don't think she's actually realised how...how unstable Clarissa's behaviour was,' Tania told him carefully as they went upstairs. 'Children don't, you know. They tend to accept adult behaviour as being different from their own. All she said to me was that when you arrived Clarissa cried a lot.'

'Really? Well, I suppose that's one way of describing it.'

The grim expression in his eyes gave way to one of such haunting despair that Tania moved instinctively towards him, her hand reaching out to touch his jacket-clad arm in a gesture of sympathy and understanding.

Briefly she felt him tense beneath her touch and her face flamed with embarrassment and self-consciousness, but as she started to move away he covered her hand with his own, holding it where it was as though he wanted the physical contact with her.

'I keep going over and over the whole thing in my mind... walking into the house, seeing your daughter there... thinking...' He shook his head. 'God help me, for a moment I thought you'd actually... And then Clarissa came in and started talking wildly about how she'd make you sorry... how she'd make you give up Nicholas, and even then I didn't realise. Not until she started saying that I'd have to help her to hide Lucy away somewhere where no one could find her.

'I blame myself entirely. I should have realised. She's always been too highly strung. There was a brief breakdown when our parents were killed.' He shook his head tiredly. 'But that was nearly fifteen years ago. I never thought... I suppose I didn't *want* to think.

'Fortunately Nicholas arrived home just as I was trying to explain to her that I had to bring Lucy back to you. He told me everything. Admitted that he'd deliberately pretended the two of you were having an affair. Apparently Clarissa's behaviour has steadily been growing more and more out of control, but I've put it down to dissatisfaction with their marriage. To resentment, if you like, and because of that I'd tended to cover up for her out of a mixture of love and pride.

'Obviously it can't go on. We called the doctor before I left. He knows of a private clinic in London where they specialise in dealing with cases like Clarissa's. It could take some time, but with careful counselling and control there's every possibility that her mental condition can be stabilised.'

'It must have been a shock for you,' Tania murmured, not knowing what else she could say.

It was plain that what had happened had affected him very deeply, otherwise she was sure he would never be unburdening himself to her in the way that it was. It was as though in some strange way the day's trauma had united them, drawing them together from their opposite sides of the chasm which had separated them, uniting them in a common bond of anguish and shock.

'You could say that, although when I think what you must have been through today, what *you* must have endured . . .'

'Oddly it never occurred to me that Clarissa might be responsible for Lucy's disappearance, although in the circumstances . . .'

'It was an impulse decision, apparently. She was driving down the street, saw Lucy on her own——'

'Which was my fault. I had intended to go and meet her, only a customer came into the shop. It doesn't matter how many times you hear of some horrible fate overtaking a child, there are always times when for one reason or another you can't be there with them. When something like this happens it brings home all the more, that there but for the grace of God...'

She swallowed hard, her throat burning with tears, closing her eyes against them and then opening them in shock when she felt James's free hand comfortingly stroking her skin, easing the tension from her muscles as he slid his hand under her hair and gently massaged the back of her neck.

'If anything had happened to Lucy, I'd never have forgiven myself. What makes it worse is that I've aided and abetted Clarissa in her delusions about your supposed affair,' he told her huskily.

'That wasn't your fault. Nicholas should have told you the truth. I told him I wanted him to. It was a stupid idea, and I was angry with him for involving me.'

'That makes two of us. Before we go any further I want to apologise to you personally. I should have used reason and logic instead of blindly giving in to my emotions.'

'You weren't entirely to blame. Clarissa *is* your sister, after all. It's natural that you should want to protect her, that your emotional response to her anxiety——'

'It wasn't my emotional response to *Clarissa* that caused me to over-react so intensely,' he interrupted rawly.

Tania tensed, her eyes widening slightly as she searched his face.

'That first time we met, I had come here to reason with you, to ask you calmly and quietly to think about what you were doing... to appeal to you, if you like, to put an end to your relationship with Nicholas before it was too late.'

'You actually consider trying to bribe me into ending the "affair" reasonable?' Tania asked drily.

'No, I don't. And it was not what I intended to do at all, but I took one look at you and quite honestly everything I'd planned to say... to do went right out of my head.'

'I did rather get the feeling you'd taken an instant dislike to me,' Tania agreed as lightly as she could. His hand was still resting on her nape, the slow movement of his fingers now not so much soothing as distinctly disturbing. If she didn't fight to keep her mind distracted she could all too easily fall into the trap of wondering what it would be like to have his fingers... his hands caressing her entire body.

'Dislike?'

His voice had an odd rough note in it. 'Is that what you *really* thought? No, it wasn't dislike that made me so aggressive. It was desire... desire and sheer bloody male jealousy. I took one look at you and I wanted you so badly that the thought of you being involved with any other man—never mind my own brother-in-law—nearly drove me out of my mind. To my shame, it wasn't so much a need to protect Clarissa's marriage that drove me but my need to separate you from Nicholas so that you'd be free...' He broke off, shaking his head tiredly.

'I shouldn't be burdening you with all this. Not now of all times. But men of my age become notoriously maudlin when they fall in love. We don't expect it, you see. We think we know all there is to know about the human race, especially when it comes to our own reactions. We think we're too mature, too sensible to be caught up in the kind of emotional maelstrom we believe is reserved only for teenagers. That's why it hits us so hard. Why we react so... so stupidly.'

James, in love with her. It couldn't be true—but before she could say so, he was telling her softly, 'You shouldn't let me be here alone with you like this, you know. You should send me away before this whole situation gets completely out of hand and I do something we'll both regret.'

Maybe he was right, but it was impossible for her to think straight, to analyse and behave logically when her brain was still trying to accept what he had told her, and she was subtly and weakeningly becoming aware that there was somehow less space between their bodies than there had been and that she could feel the heat coming from his; that heat was like a silent command whispered to her own body, causing it to react to him as immediately and obviously as though he had commanded its response out loud.

'Tell me to leave, Tania,' he demanded unsteadily. 'Otherwise...'

Tell him to *leave*. But that was the last thing she wanted him to do. She *wanted* to be with him. She *needed* to be with him. She *had* to be with him, she recognised as she impulsively closed the distance between them and raised her face for his kiss.

The first real kiss she had ever received, she realised shakily minutes later, when her lips were still clinging softly to his, her heartbeat suffocatingly loud in her ears, mirroring the erotic thud of her pulse.

It was as though the trauma of the day had set her free from the bonds of convention and caution, as though something inside her was telling her to reach out and take what she was being offered; and more, much more, there was a need in her to lift the burden of guilt and pain from James's shoulders, a need to respond to the sharp clarity of the only truth that mattered: that here was a man whom she wanted and desired, a man she could well even love, and, if the immediacy of their physical coming together here tonight was something which society and convention might judge and condemn, that didn't matter to her. What did matter was that life was suddenly offering her a chance to experience something she had thought she never would experience, that now after all these years she was being given a chance to fulfil herself as a woman and she knew that if she ignored her need, if she ignored his need, she would regret it for the rest of her life. It was meant to be...ordained almost if such a thought were not profane.

As James reluctantly released her mouth, he whispered against her lips, 'If you want me to go...?'

Immediately her arms tightened betrayingly around him.

'No...no, I don't.'

Somehow or other she managed to stand still when he framed her face with his hands and searched her expression with deep intensity.

'Is it the same for you, then?' he asked her softly.

Which of them was trembling, or was it both of them?

'I think so,' she admitted shakily. 'I'm not used to this kind of thing. There hasn't——'

'Not even with Lucy's father.'

Immediately she froze. Keeping her voice as steady as she could, she told him flatly, 'Lucy's father virtually raped me. It was partly my own fault. I had no idea... I was so naïve...and, to be fair to him, I don't think he realised how inexperienced I actually was.'

James was frowning now, distancing himself a little from her.

If her admission, her honesty had made him withdraw from her, then so be it, she reflected painfully. There had been enough misunderstandings between them, enough half-truths and lies. He was obviously a sexually experienced man; if he expected her experience to match his own, then it was better that he knew the truth. If he rejected her because of her inexperience...

'And how inexperienced were you?' he asked her carefully, watching her.

'Completely.'

'And since then?'

'Since then...' She hesitated for a fraction of a second, looking down at the floor and then back up at him as she admitted honestly, 'Since then I haven't had either the time or the inclination to become involved either sexually or emotionally. Much less with a married man with two children.'

For a moment he was so silent that she panicked and wondered if she had said too much, admitted too much. He was an intelligent man. It wouldn't take a great deal of deduction to work out that since she had been celibate for so long her willingness, her eagerness for this intimacy with him betrayed far more than a casual, fleeting need to appease the physical hunger of a sexually experienced body.

'I *have* maligned you, haven't I?' he said rawly at last.

'If it puts you off...my lack of...of experience——' Tania whispered hesitantly.

'Puts me off...' He groaned and slid his hands down her back to her bottom, moulding her against his body so that she could feel its arousal. 'I doubt that anything could put me off you. I learned a long time ago that sex for sex's sake has no meaning for me, no real pleasure. I've never yet made love with a woman I haven't respected and liked as well as desired, but I'd long ago given up believing that I'd ever meet a woman I could love. Until I met you.' He lifted one hand from her body and traced the shape of her half-parted mouth with his fingertip.

'You can't imagine what it did to my self-respect to realise that I'd fallen in love with a woman who apparently was the complete opposite of all the things I've always believed a woman—my woman—would be. I should have known better, trusted my instincts... Do you love me, Tania?'

'I don't know,' she admitted huskily, her mouth trembling, her tongue tripping her up a little as she stumbled over the admission. 'I know I need you, I want you... That's hard enough for me to accept. I'm not used... I never thought...'

'I shouldn't rush you... I should wait.'

'No,' she denied fiercely. 'No.' She looked at him, her eyes appealing to him, full of all the words she couldn't bring herself to say.

'Yes,' he said at last, as though in answer to a spoken question. 'Perhaps tonight was meant to be...a catharsis for both of us. Although...' He frowned suddenly as she looked questioningly, trustingly up to him.

'What?'

'Nothing,' he told her softly, smiling down at her. 'Nothing at all.'

Suddenly she felt slightly awkward, ill at ease and uncertain, not sure what to do. Would he expect her to suggest they went to her bedroom?

Silently she cursed her previously unregretted lack of experience. What was the done thing in such circumstances? This was *her* home. She was a mature adult woman, who had had no qualms about admitting that she wanted to make love with him, so why did she now experience this reluctance, this reticence?

'Tania.'

The sound of her name made her look up at him. He took hold of her hand as he smiled down at her, linking his fingers through hers.

His grip was strong and firm, safe.

'You don't have to do this, you know,' he told her quietly. 'Not unless you want to.'

'I want to,' she assured him shakily, knowing that it was true. 'I want to,' she repeated with a wry laugh. 'But that doesn't stop me being scared to death.'

'Does it help to know that I'm scared too?'

She stared at him and queried disbelievingly, 'You?'

'Mm. I want so much to please you, to give you all that you've never known, and I'm terrified that if I don't . . . if I can't, that you'll turn away from me.'

His mouth was just a breath away from her own. She had an overwhelming need to reach up and claim it. As though he sensed what she was feeling, he bent his head, feathering her mouth with his.

Immediately a surge of pleasure swamped her, her lips parting beneath his in blind, instinctive need.

'Tania.'

She moaned softly deep in her throat as he pulled her closer to his body, her hips moving automatically, eagerly against him.

She wanted his kiss never to end. Her starved senses soaked up the sensations he was arousing inside her like parched earth absorbing much-needed rain.

When his hands swept up over her back and under her arms, she moved instinctively, easing her body away from his so that his hands could cup her breasts.

She might never have known these sensations before, but her body certainly recognised them, welcomed them, hungered for them, she realised dizzily, her breathing a stifled whimper of anguished need and disappointment as James removed his hands from her body.

'Shush... It's all right,' he told her, pushing her hair back off her face with tender fingers, soothing her with a kiss that began as a gentle caress of reassurance but quickly hardened to urgent desire as he felt her eager response.

When she felt him unfastening the buttons on her shirt, her whole body went tense with excitement. Long before he had laid bare the soft, pale skin of her breasts, her nipples were taut with arousal, her throat and face flushed with the need that pulsed so strongly inside her.

The way he looked at her, the way he touched her made her catch her breath in a mingling of pain and pride. He made no attempt to conceal his emotional response to the intimacy between them. No man had ever touched her like this before, and neither had she ever thought she would want one to, and yet when James sank down into the armchair behind him, pulling her down on to his lap, his breath warm against her naked skin, she felt such a tumult of sensation inside her that it was all she could do not to imprison his head with her hands and urge him to take the pulsing eagerness of her breasts into his mouth.

He seemed to know just what it was she wanted, though, caressing first the taut line of her throat, pausing at its base for a second while her heart kicked beneath his hand and her body trembled with eagerness and need.

When he cupped her breast with his hand and gently ran his thumb over its hard centre, she moaned out loud, the sharp sound dying abruptly as he bent his head and lovingly took her erect nipple into the moist paradise of his mouth.

She had never dreamed there could be such a feeling, such a need, such a torment that was so intense...so immediate...so far out of her control that she could do nothing other than clutch at the soft darkness of his hair with fingers suddenly rigid and tense as her heartbeat accelerated to a more frantic drumming.

The sweet torment of his long slow suckling of first one breast and then the other brought down the last of her emotional barriers. No man who did not love her could have caressed her like this. And no man she did not love in return could have aroused her so immediately and so intensely.

When he finally raised his head from her glistening breasts, she heard him mutter raggedly into her throat, 'My God, you're like no other woman I've ever known. You do things to me.'

She felt him shudder and immediately wrapped her arms around him in the eternal feminine gesture of strength and knowledge, savouring her awareness that in her arms he was as weak, as vulnerable as a mere child, and yet at the same time... As she moved against him and felt his arousal, her body melted and ached inside, yearned and demanded.

He moved slightly away from her, taking off his jacket and his shirt.

His chest was broad and tanned, his arms hard with strong muscles that her fingertips just ached to explore. In the lamplight she could see that dark cross of hair that bisected his chest horizontally and tapered diagonally from his breastbone to where it disappeared beneath his belt.

'Stop looking at me like that,' he told her unevenly as he gathered her back in his arms, easing her down against him, kissing her fiercely, his chest expanding and pushing against the softness of her breasts so that their tenderness was intensified by the urgent movement of his body against her own.

Wrapped in an invisible blanket of languid pleasure, she lay motionless and bemused as he undressed her, watching with appreciative, fascinated eyes as he quickly removed his own clothes and lifted her gently down on to the floor where he lay down beside her.

When she reached out instinctively to touch him, he stopped her, gathering both her hands in his and kissing her open palms.

'No, not yet,' he told her thickly. 'If you do...'

As his body shuddered, her own trembled in response. Still holding her hands, he bent his head and kissed the soft roundness of her belly.

She drew in her breath automatically, startled by the thrill of sensation that ran through her, at her body's uninhibited eagerness to offer itself up to deeper intimacies.

But even as she tried to check that small betraying arch of her spine, that tiny quiver that convulsed her, James had released her hands and was covering the soft-fleshed mound of her femininity with one hand while the other slid beneath her and his lips moved eagerly over her tender skin, refusing to allow her to deny him the intimacy he wanted.

The sensation of him touching her there, at the most intimate heart of her body, was so fiercely pleasurable that to withstand the exquisite sensation flooding through her was impossible.

As her body writhed in helpless abandonment to his touch she cried out his name, wanting him, aching for him, reaching for him, wrapping herself eagerly around him as he kissed his way back up her body to her mouth, telling her hoarsely how much he wanted her as he lifted her against him and entered her gently but determinedly.

Had he guessed how apprehensive she was about this; how vulnerable to his physical possession? As she opened her eyes and looked wonderingly at him, he told her rawly, 'It's all right. I'm not going to hurt you. If you want me to stop you only have to say.'

If she wanted him to stop? His body moved within her own and her fear fell away drowned by the tide of sensation that rolled through her.

She might never have experienced this kind of sensation before, might have never known that it existed, but her body, her senses, seemed to know instinctively how to respond to it.

She could feel the heavy, uneven thud of James's heartbeat, hear the harsh rasp of each shuddering indrawn breath, feel the growing tension and need within his body, a need and tension echoed deep within her own flesh, a driven aching need for fulfilment that made her turn her head frantically from side to side, her fingers digging into his skin as she arched up against him, inciting him to increase the fierce driving rhythm that was now the focus of her whole world.

An awareness that such need, such intensity could not be endured for too long made her cry out imploringly to him, a jumble of words which made no logical sense and yet at the same time which said everything.

And then unbelievably, suddenly, she was there in that special place she had heard about, read about, and always privately felt she would never experience, and the joy and the wonder of it brought tears to her eyes and clamped tight her throat so that while James shuddered helplessly against her all she could do was bury her face against his throat and hold him tight in a wordless gesture of delight, awe and exhaustion.

When he turned her gently on to her side and wrapped her tenderly in his arms, kissing her softly and lingeringly, she felt as boneless and fluid as a length of silk, as feline and replete as a basking cat, and fulfilled in a way she had never dreamed possible for anyone, never mind imagined experiencing herself.

'I want to spend the night with you,' James told her softly. 'I want to wake up with you in my arms.

To know that this wasn't all just an illusion, an impossible fantasy. But perhaps not this time. There's Lucy to consider.'

Sleepily she nodded her head. Yes, there was Lucy to consider and, delightful though the prospect of waking up with him next to her in the morning was, common sense and caution warned her against giving in to such an impulse.

And besides, right now . . . right now she felt far too bemused, far too complete . . . far too . . . She yawned hugely and closed her eyes and almost instantly was deeply asleep.

As he felt her body relax in his arms, James looked down at her.

It had hit him so unexpectedly, so unwantedly, this need for her, this desire, this overwhelming tide of emotion and hunger.

He knew he had rushed her, perhaps even using a time of great emotional vulnerability and anxiety against her; taking advantage of it to draw her into a deeper intimacy than she would otherwise have allowed him.

And he had made love to her without taking any precautions to protect her from an unplanned and unwanted pregnancy.

Soberly he studied her. How would she feel when she woke up?

He wished he could stay with her, but he had promised Nicholas that he would be waiting for him when he returned from the clinic.

He sighed, feeling the first sharp knifing of a resentment against both his brother-in-law and against Clarissa herself in her possessive dependence on him.

She would not easily accept the existence of another woman in his life, especially not one who was more important to him than she was herself. And especially not this woman.

CHAPTER EIGHT

TANIA awoke to the most glorious sense of well-being she could ever remember experiencing in her life. She stretched languorously and lazily beneath the bedclothes before she realised just where the lovely sensation of hedonistic relaxation came from. Then she tensed and looked wildly around her bedroom as though expecting James to suddenly materialise out of thin air.

James... James Warren had come here last night and she... She sat bolt upright, hugging her arms protectively around her knees and took a deep breath. There was no use trying to hide from it. Last night she and James Warren had been lovers.

Lovers... She shivered a little at the easy, tempting way the word slid into her mind... And yet... and yet to describe what had happened between them as merely sex was neither honest nor fair, she recognised. Theirs had not been a mere casual sexual encounter to be quickly brushed aside and forgotten.

James had been open and honest with her about his feelings, about his desire for her. And she... She shivered again, unable to remember exactly what she might or might not have verbally betrayed to him during the intense emotional heat of their passion.

All she could remember was that James had made it plain to her that he wanted a continuing relationship with her. He had fallen in love with her, he had said. She started to shake, tears suddenly filling her eyes. Oh, God, what was happening to her? She had known the first moment she saw him how dangerously attracted she was to him, but then she had never dreamed... never imagined that he had been equally aware of her.

But last night he had told her, shown her. Last night should never have happened, she berated herself guiltily. What on earth had happened to her normal caution and reserve? Why, she had practically invited him to make love to her... virtually insisted and begged...

'Mum! Is it time to get up yet? And can I go round and see Susan? I want to tell her all about the puppy James is going to give me.'

Quickly rubbing away her tears, Tania forced herself to respond easily and lightly to Lucy's good morning hug. Fortunately her daughter appeared to have emerged from what could have been a traumatic and haunting experience with no apparent after-effects, and it would be foolish of her to start behaving in an emotional and possibly alarming way towards Lucy, just because she was so conscious of how easily her precious child could have been hurt physically and emotionally, perhaps even permanently damaged by Clarissa Forbes's jealousy. If James hadn't gone round to see his sister when he had... If... If she hadn't stopped to serve that woman, but had gone to meet Lucy as she had said she would... If Clarissa hadn't seen her walking alone in the street ... If ... So many ifs, but there was no point in torturing herself and possibly upsetting Lucy by dwelling on them. It was enough that she would have to spend the rest of her life carrying the burden of knowing how vulnerable Lucy had been.

Well, from now on she intended to make sure that Lucy's safety was never put at risk in that way again. From now on ...

As Lucy wriggled away from her she heard her saying excitedly, 'I haven't chosen a name for the puppy yet, Mummy. I'm going to ask James what he thinks. I like him, don't you?'

'What?'

Tania focused on Lucy's bright, happy face.

'James, Mum.' Lucy repeated patiently. 'I like him.'

'Yes ... yes he's very nice,' Tania agreed automatically. James had saved her daughter's life. Had been there for Lucy to protect her from harm when she herself had not. An odd ache, a strange tug of emotion which was both gratitude and a little resentment ... a little jealousy pulled at her heart. She had seen the obvious affection and trust that Lucy felt for James when he had first brought her home. Had seen it and had somehow felt excluded from it.

Was that what had driven her so precipitately into James' arms? Was that why ...?

She turned her head to gaze unfocusedly out of her bedroom window.

Why not admit it? she derided herself inwardly. You're hopelessly, helplessly, totally, idiotically in love with the man, and you know it.

'Mum.' Lucy was shaking her arm impatiently. 'When are you going to get up? I'm hungry and I want to go round and tell Susie about my puppy.'

'I'm getting up now,' Tania assured her, but she couldn't stop herself from adding protectively, 'I don't think it would be a good idea to go round to Susan's today, poppet.'

Instantly Lucy's face fell as she protested, 'But, Mum...'

The phone rang before Tania could speak. As she picked up the receiver she knew her heart had started to pound far too fast. Her hand felt cold and clammy, and her voice when she said the number was high and very strained.

'Tania, it's Ann. I just thought I'd give you a ring and see how you're feeling.'

Ann. Her heart plummeted downwards like a sky diver without a parachute, the sickness of disappointment knotting her stomach. Stupid of her to have assumed that it must be James.

'I'm fine. We both are,' Tania told her, forcing herself to smile so that her friend would not pick up the disappointment she was feeling. 'I'll tell you all about it, but not now. It seems Clarissa Forbes happened to see Lucy walking down the street and picked her up. James found her there when he went round to see Clarissa. He said that Clarissa has had some kind of breakdown.'

'A breakdown? The woman must be totally insane to do a thing like that!' Ann expostulated acidly. 'How's Lucy?'

'Bright as a button, with no apparent after-effects,' Tania told her wryly. 'James has promised her a puppy and she seems more concerned about that than anything else.'

'Susie keeps asking when she can see her.'

'Not today,' Tania told her quickly, and then added huskily, 'I feel as though I can hardly bear to let her out of my sight at the moment.' She spoke softly, keeping her voice low so that Lucy, who was at the other side of the room, couldn't hear her.

'Well, that's understandable enough,' Ann responded gently. 'But for Lucy's sake perhaps it would be better not to fuss over her too much. If she isn't showing any after-effects...'

Sensible advice, but not the advice Tania really wanted to hear. She had an atavistic, deep-rooted need to keep her daughter as close to her side as possible. It would be a long time before the events of yesterday were something she could remember without terror, if ever.

Having assured Ann that she would be sending Lucy to school in the morning as usual, she said goodbye and replaced the receiver.

Would James ring her? Would he perhaps come and see her? And if he did, what would he say to her... or she to him? What had seemed so perfect, so natural last night, now this morning seemed to have been an alien, bewildering act on her part; something she had never even remotely imagined herself doing, the kind of intimacy which was surely too much; far too fast.

And yet... And yet... even as the thoughts formed, her body, as though rebelling against them, gave a tiny little shiver, reminding her of the pleasure James had shown her, had given her, had shared with her, and a weakening wave of tenderness and longing swept over her.

An hour later, breakfast over, Lucy resigned if not altogether happy about the fact that they would be spending the entire day together, she was trying to coax her daughter into a more enthusiastic frame of mind about how they could best spend the day, when Lucy, who had been looking out of the sitting-room window, suddenly cried out excitedly, 'It's James, Mum, James is here!'

Immediately Tania leapt out of her chair and rushed over to the window, stopping abruptly before she got there, her face flushed as she chewed frantically on her bottom lip, torn between apprehension and delight.

James here. What was she going to say to him? What was he going to say to her? She stood uncertainly where she was. How awful if he had caught her rushing over to the window to gaze at him like a lovesick teenager, and yet when she heard him ring their private doorbell at the rear entrance to the building her heart pounded as idiotically as though she were that age.

'I'll go and let him in,' Lucy announced excitedly, bounding out of the room before she could stop her.

She heard Lucy chattering enthusiastically to him as they came up the stairs, and suddenly wished despairingly that she were wearing something more sophisticated than her old worn jeans and the baggy sweatshirt with the Mickey Mouse motif on it which Lucy had chosen for her.

She kept her back to the door as Lucy pushed it open, cravenly trying to pretend she was engrossed in the newspaper article she was trying to read.

'Mum, James wants us to go to his house and have lunch with him there,' Lucy announced excitedly as she burst into the room.

She dropped the paper, the words of denial springing to her lips, her emotions immediately shying away from the intimacy Lucy's words conjured up, but even as she started to make the denial she was looking at him and seeing the lines of strain and anxiety tensing his face, and her resistance, her apprehension, her doubts melted in the heat that suddenly filled her.

'I would have been here earlier,' he was telling her huskily, 'but there were things we had to do. Formalities to attend to. The police have agreed not to make any charges against Clarissa for the time being, pending her specialist's report on her mental condition.

'Nicholas and I both went to see him this morning. It's just as well the boys are back at school.' He looked so grave, so worn down that somehow she was beside him, placing her hand comfortingly on his arm.

Unlike her he was formally dressed; in a dark suit, a crisp white shirt, a sober tie, almost like a man wearing mourning, she reflected as she studied the shadows and hollows of his face.

'The specialist believes she *will* recover, given time. It's come to light that there was some sort of minor crisis when Clive was born, but I was away at the time, and the doctor put it down to post-baby blues. However, now, with hindsight, the specialist feels that it could have been the trigger for this latest attack.'

'But Clive is seven years old.'

'I know, but in the specialist's view...' He shrugged almost helplessly.

Tania forced herself to ask him, 'And Clarissa, how is she in herself?'

She knew that it was only her love for him, her compassion for and aching understanding of all that he wasn't saying, but which she could see written so clearly in his eyes, that made her ask the question.

Right now she was finding it hard to summon up much sympathy for Clarissa. All she could think was how easily James's stepsister might have harmed her own child.

'Deeply sedated at the moment, and for some time to come. I thought you and Lucy might like to come back to Dove Court and have lunch with me. Rupert is there,' he added for Lucy's benefit, explaining tiredly to Tania, 'I offered to take charge of him for Nicholas. He's going to have enough on his plate what with his work and visiting both Clarissa and the boys. Of course, I'll be sharing the visiting with him. Luckily I haven't any overseas trips planned at the moment, and I can shift my work around so that I can spend some time with Clarissa during the day when Nicholas is working.'

Tania didn't like the jealousy that filled her as she listened to these plans. Of course he would want to visit his stepsister, to make sure she was receiving the very best of treatment. She must not forget that James loved Clarissa, just as she loved Lucy.

But James was not Clarissa's father, she told herself rebelliously and a little bitterly. There wasn't even any real blood relationship between them.

Which surely made James's concern for her all the more praiseworthy. She had no right to feel jealous, to feel angry almost as though in wanting to see his stepsister James was somehow being disloyal to her.

However, it was one thing to tell herself logically she was being both unfair and a little ridiculous; it was another thing altogether to translate these admirable thoughts into an emotion strong enough to wipe out the dark feelings possessing her.

'It's very good of you to call,' she told him coolly, ignoring the way his expression changed, weariness giving way to a sharp look of disquiet, of pain almost as she added curtly, 'Unfortunately I'm afraid we shan't be able to have lunch with you. I've already turned down an invitation from Ann Fielding and quite honestly, I feel that for the moment, I want to spend as much time as possible with Lucy. Just the two of us.'

The tiny shiver she gave wasn't forced, nor was the sudden shadowing of her eyes, or the way her hands trembled, and she saw from the way that he

was looking at her that James knew quite well what
had caused them.

'I'm more sorry than I can say about what happened with Lucy,' he told her in a low voice so that
Lucy herself could not overhear them. 'And I do
understand your need to be with her, to protect her.
But no good purpose will be served by your being
over-protective towards her. All you'll do is stifle
her, cause her——'

It was too much. Tania turned on him immediately, snapping bitterly, 'How dare you accuse *me*
of being over protective, when you can't even admit
that you've spoiled and protected your own stepsister, a grown woman, not a child, so much that
you're the pivot for her whole life.'

She regretted the cruel words the moment she had
uttered them, and knew that it was jealousy and
fear that had drawn them from her heart like poi-
soned arrows which she had let fly at him, wanting
to wound and hurt.

He had gone pale, whether with anger or anguish
she could not tell.

'You're quite right, of course,' he told her stiffly.
'I *am* the last person to criticise, although in
Clarissa's case... Well, emotionally, mentally she
was never lucky enough to have the resilience of
your Lucy. Perhaps when you're feeling in a
more...receptive frame of mind I can tell you a
little about her background. And, before you say
it, maybe I am making excuses for her, or looking
for reasons.' His voice was toneless, hollow and
drained of all emotion as he turned away from her.
'Perhaps that's the only way I can alleviate my own

burden of guilt.' He turned back to her and demanded fiercely, 'Do you really not suppose that I have asked myself over and over again how much of this whole sorry mess is *my* fault? How much of the blame lies on my shoulders, how much of Clarissa's unfortunate weakness, her dependence, her jealousy has been, if unknowingly, fostered by me?'

He looked so tormented, so stripped of the pride and self-assurance that had seemed so much a part of him that instinctively she sought to comfort him, forgetting her own fears, her own feelings, as she placed her hand comfortingly on his arm and said shakily, 'You mustn't blame yourself.'

'Mustn't I?' His voice was self-derisive. 'How can I do otherwise?'

'Mum, when are we going to see James's house?' Lucy demanded, breaking into their conversation.

It was James who started to answer her, beginning wearily, 'Perhaps another time——'

'We're going just as soon as you've got your coat on,' Tania interrupted him quickly. 'And you can bring my jacket for me as well, please,' she called after her as Lucy rushed out of the room.

When they were on their own she looked at James and added huskily, 'That's if the invitation still stands.'

'It still stands,' James assured her.

His hands were on her arms now, drawing her close to him, his breath warm against her skin as he lowered his lips to her ear and whispered softly, 'And I still haven't told you how much last night meant to me.'

She had started to tremble. Automatically her arms went round him, holding him close, her heartbeat racing with excitement and tension, as her body recognised the heat and arousal of his.

'I want you so much,' he groaned against her ear. 'I came here today determined to behave in a mature and controlled fashion to reassure you that, while last night was the most wonderful night of my life, I could control my desire for you and take things slowly, allow you all the time you needed to get to know me, to talk things over sensibly and maturely, and yet now, with you in my arms, all I can think about is how much I want to kiss you...to touch you, to hold you the way I held you last night and to make love to you until you make those same little sounds of pleasure against my skin, until you...'

His lips were caressing her throat in between the husky words he was whispering to her. She was trembling violently, her body reacting as urgently and eagerly as his. She closed her eyes, tilting her head to one side and whimpering huskily with pleasure as his mouth devoured the exposed column of her throat. Another second or so and he would be touching her mouth, caressing it with his lips, gently at first, delicately as though she were the most delicate and precious thing on earth, and then less gently, and more passionately, far more passionately until...

'Mum, I've got your jacket.'

Her eyes opened, her body tensing as she tried automatically to step back from James, but he refused to release her so that when Lucy bounded into the room he was standing with one arm around her.

Lucy seemed completely unperturbed by their intimacy, coming over to her and handing her her jacket.

'Is Rupert really staying with you?' she asked James as they all headed downstairs.

'Yes, he is indeed,' James assured her, and then added, 'I think you and I might have a go at training him, and teaching him some sense. What do you say?'

'Oh, yes, let's,' Lucy agreed quickly, and when Tania had finished locking the door, she turned round to discover that Lucy had slipped her hand into James's and was standing gazing up at him with something very close to adoration in her eyes.

Fear clutched at Tania's stomach, fear not just for herself but for her child as well. Things were happening too quickly, and too intensely. She had no experience of this kind of thing, no previous knowledge by which she could judge the present situation. Instinct warned her to be cautious, but when James turned and looked at her and smiled at her the way he was doing right now, it was difficult to remember to be cautious, difficult to remember anything at all other than the way he made her feel when he touched her.

'No, Mum. You sit in the front with James,' Lucy instructed her firmly, when James had unlocked the car door, and settled Lucy safely in the rear seatbelt.

Confused, Tania hesitated, standing beside the rear door, until James said softly, 'Yes, Tania, you come and sit beside me. Please.'

Willingly she did so, fumbling with the seatbelt until he took it from her and gently slotted it into place, smiling at her the whole time, so that even though he hadn't actually touched her body she was sharply aware of how much he would have liked to do so, of how easily, had they been alone, he might have slid his hands over her body and caressed her breasts, as he had done last night. Her chest felt tight, her breath had become erratic, beneath her sweatshirt she felt the sudden tightening of her nipples and her face flushed with mortification. She could feel James looking at her, and prayed that he wasn't able to read her mind. That she, she who had never really experienced any kind of wanton sexual urges or impulses, should now feel this, react like this, ache like this...

She bit her lip, worrying it, believing that her thoughts, her feelings were known only to herself until James set the car in motion and told her softly, 'It's just the same for me, you know. And contrary to popular myth the majority of men do not enjoy wanting one particular woman so much that the mere thought of her is enough to bring them to intense physical arousal...especially not once they get to my age.

'Don't look at me like that,' he told her roughly, when she turned towards him, an involuntary protest on her lips, even while her eyes were rounding with shocked excitement. 'Don't,' he repeated. 'Otherwise there's no way I'm going to be able to keep my hands off you.'

Why was it that her body reacted to his words more as though they were a promise than a threat?

Trying to fight against the sensations quivering inside her she turned round to ask Lucy if she was all right, all too conscious of her flushed skin and husky voice.

Perhaps it was because she had never experienced passion before, never imagined it could ever be something she would know at first hand, never believed or considered that she would want with such intensity that she was so bowled over by what she was feeling, alternately bewildered and bemused by it, torn between awed delight and sharp fear as she recognised how drastically, how permanently what she was feeling was going to change her life. There was no going back now, no way she could wipe out what had happened and return to her safe, unawakened state. Even if she never saw James again, even if she shut him out of her life completely, she could never obliterate the memories he had given her; the feelings, the emotions, the needs. No, she would never be able to wipe her emotions or her body free of their knowledge of him.

She felt the car slowing down and turned her head, focusing on her surroundings. They were turning in through a minute pair of gate lodges, shaped like dovecotes.

'Hence the name of the house,' James told her wryly, aware of her small start of pleasure. 'Not original features of the house, though. That was built in sixteen hundred and odd. These were added round about eighteen-fifty when the estate was bought by the first Warren to settle here. He apparently built them to please his new bride. Perhaps after all I oughtn't to be so surprised at the way I'm reacting to you. It isn't as though I'm the first Warren male to fall helplessly and very deeply in love.'

Lucy wasn't listening to them; she was too busy exclaiming her excitement as James drove down the long gravel drive. The lawns that swept back from it were covered in fallen leaves from the trees that lined the drives and dotted the green parkland, many of them probably rare specimens, Tania reflected, trying not to give in to her growing awe.

When she had glimpsed the house from the river, she had not realised it might be so impressive, so stately, and it was almost a relief when they rounded the final bend and she saw the house in front of her to realise that it was not after all the imposing edifice she had been dreading, but rather a delightful creeper-clad three-storeyed building of simple proportions built in what she later discovered was a classic H shape out of soft russet-coloured bricks.

James stopped the car, allowing her to study the house in silence until Lucy exclaimed impatiently, 'Where's Rupert? Can I play outside with him, please, James?'

'After your mother and I have had a cup of tea, we'll all go for a walk through the grounds,' James promised her, and then, turning to Tania, he said simply and quietly, 'Welcome to what I hope one day very soon will become your new home, Tania, my beloved.'

CHAPTER NINE

Tears stung Tania's eyes. She reached shakily for the seatbelt release, letting her hair slide forward protectively to conceal her expression from James.

This place her home? Nothing could have been a greater contrast to her inner city flat, and yet instead of feeling awed or intimidated as she walked with James into the magnificent tiled hallway she felt as though the house were actually welcoming her.

The soft sounds of creaking wood, the scent of beeswax polish from the panelling, and apple logs from the open fire; all of them were somehow familiar and warming. It was as though the house itself were murmuring its appreciation of her, settling warmly around her.

On the polished oak table next to the huge jug of autumn flowers stood a large silver framed photograph. She focused on it automatically, catching her breath as she recognised a much, much younger James standing between an older man and woman. The young girl standing at his side must surely be Clarissa.

As though he sensed what she was thinking, James moved over to the table and picked up the photograph.

'My father and Clarissa's mother shortly after they were married. He'd been a very lonely man after my mother's death and Harriet made him very, very happy——'

He was about to say something else, but broke off as they heard a sharp volley of shrill barks from behind one of the doors. Someone opened it from the other side, and Rupert came rushing out to greet them all with ecstatic, enthusiastic barks and licks.

The plump, rather breathless woman following him apologised, 'I am sorry, Mr Warren, but he was that excited.'

'Don't worry about it, Jane. While you're here let me introduce you to Ms Carter and her daughter, Lucy.'

He drew Tania forward, standing behind her, with his hands placed lightly and yet very possessively on her shoulders as she shook hands with the older woman.

As he introduced her to Jane Williams, his housekeeper, Tania reflected ruefully that he was making their relationship more than plain to the older woman, but if she was either surprised by or disapproving of it she did not betray it in the genuinely warm and welcoming smile she gave Tania, before turning to Lucy and exclaiming with pleasure, 'So this is the young lady who is going to take this rascal Rupert out of my kitchen for a little while.'

'I'm afraid Jane is finding Rupert something of a trial,' James told Tania after the housekeeper had excused herself to finish preparing lunch. 'It isn't that she's anti-animal, far from it. The kitchen is in fact ruled by an extremely large and lazy cat which she spoils to death, but Rupert's manners leave something to be desired, I'm afraid to say. I said to Clarissa when she bought him that she'd be better off with a more placid breed, a retriever or a labrador, but no, she'd set her heart on having a King Charles, and, quite irresponsibly, totally refused to make any attempt to train him. It's not the dog's fault. He had a nice enough nature, but he's already caused a commotion locally by escaping and putting up some of the birds Colonel Walters was raising for his annual shoot. Prior to that he nearly drowned himself chasing ducks in the mill pond at Mill House.'

'Can you train him, or is it too late?' Tania asked him. Now that they were alone, Lucy having gone with Jane to the kitchen to see the aforementioned cat, she suddenly felt unbearably self-conscious and nervous.

'No, it's not too late,' James told her and then came towards her, stopping a few feet short of her, to ask her gently, 'What is it? Are you really so frightened of me?'

She shook her head immediately, half laughing at her own vulnerability as she admitted, 'No, not of *you*. But I am frightened of...well, of everything else.'

For a moment he obviously didn't understand. He frowned and looked around the pleasant sitting-room in which they were standing and asked quietly, 'The house. The house frightens you?'

'No, not the house. This...this thing between us.' She still could not bring herself to put her emotions into words, to say as he had done that she loved him. 'It's all happened so quickly, so unexpectedly.'

He came to her, and took hold of her hands, holding them firmly in his own.

'Are you trying to tell me you've had second thoughts? That you don't want me? That last night——?'

'No,' she interrupted him honestly. 'It's not that. I may not have your experience, I may not have had any previous experience at all really, but I know that...' She paused, took a deep breath, looked up at him and admitted openly, 'I know that what we had...what we shared last night was something very special, something...something rare and precious, and I can't regret it. But there are so many problems, so much...'

'You're thinking about Clarissa?' he asked her.

Slowly Tania nodded her head. She hadn't wanted to voice her doubts, her apprehensions. She hadn't wanted to reveal to him what she considered to be her own small-mindedness, but she felt as though her own deep-rooted antagonism towards Clarissa was like a tiny speck of poison, so small now that one could hardly believe it could ever in any remote way harm the way she felt about him, and yet at the same time instinct told her that it was something that did threaten any future happiness they might otherwise share, and that in burying it, in ignoring it she would be allowing it to grow and fester.

Clarissa was James's stepsister. He had always loved and protected her. It was only natural that he should be concerned for her, should even make excuses for her, and Tania doubted if she would ever be totally able to come to terms with his love for her, or with his need to protect her. Just as she doubted that Clarissa would ever be able to accept another woman, any other woman in her brother's life.

Privately she didn't know if she had the temperament, the patience or the compassion to deal with Clarissa's dangerous and neurotic behaviour, and then even if she was prepared to do so, to make herself tolerate and accept Clarissa's role in James' life, how could she even think of allowing Lucy to be exposed to her venom a second time?

Much as she wanted James, much as she loved him, ached for him, needed him, how could there really be a future for them together when Clarissa would always be there between them? Even if she was the kind of woman who could ask him to banish Clarissa from his life, even if he was the kind of man who was prepared to do so, how could any kind of deep and lasting love grow between them if she forced him to make that kind of decision? How could she live with herself if she did so, never mind expect James to live with her and love her? And yet how could they have any chance of building a life together, a secure safe life for their love, for Lucy and for the children they themselves might have if Clarissa was always there, constantly reminding her of what had happened, of how she had threatened Lucy's safety?

It was a problem to which there was no answer, and now, seeing the anguish and pain in James's eyes, she whispered achingly through numb lips, 'Can't you see I have to think of Lucy...the risk?'

'Yes. Yes,' James agreed heavily. 'I *can* see that. But Tania...please let me explain about Clarissa. Sit down for a moment.'

Reluctantly Tania did so, her eyes wary as James led her to the comfortably cushioned and plump settee with its soft brocade cover, the fabric rich and warm beneath her fingertips. He sat down next to her, taking hold of her free hand and keeping it within his own.

'Clarissa's father deserted Clarissa's mother when she was seven years old. Prior to that he had treated Harriet abysmally, even to the point of trying to turn Clarissa against her mother. When he finally left the family to go and live with a woman who had been his lover for a number of years Clarissa was heartbroken, so much so that Harriet actually feared for her life. At first Clarissa blamed her mother totally for her father's absence, and then apparently she began to blame herself; to believe that it was because of something she had done wrong that her father had to her mind rejected her.

'I don't think any adult can really understand what goes on inside a vulnerable child's mind, can really know the damage that we selfishly cause when we ignore the claims of emotions of those children and allow our own feelings, our own needs to take priority.

'Apparently Clarissa became very withdrawn emotionally, going from refusing to accept that her father had actually gone, to refusing to allow his name to be mentioned in her hearing. Even years later when her mother married my father, she still couldn't bear to hear her father's name mentioned. She never saw him again after he left her mother. He remarried and went to live abroad.

'When she came here to live she seemed to attach herself to me. I felt heartily sorry for her—I'd lost my own mother, but I'd been older, known more about the world...and I'd lost her in a different way. There wasn't the same sense of betrayal as Clarissa had experienced.

'Perhaps with hindsight I *did* allow her to become too attached to me, too dependent on me, but, as with all these things, by the time I saw the danger the damage was done and it was too late to draw back without hurting Clarissa desperately, without, in her eyes at least, deserting her as her father had done. That was why I was so anxious that you shouldn't break up her marriage. I knew how vulnerable she was, how...'

'Yes,' Tania agreed shakily. 'I do understand. But understanding doesn't change anything, James,' she told him sadly. 'It doesn't alter the fact that we both know that Clarissa will always resent any other woman you take into your life, and in my case——'

'You want me to cut her out of my life, to——'

'No,' she told him vehemently, angry that he should think her so selfish. 'No, of course I don't. How could you? No. I'm not asking anything from you. Or, at least, not anything like that. What I *am* asking is that you let me go. That you let me go now, before it's too late and I don't have any will or ability to go. I'm just as capable of reacting emotionally or feeling jealousy as Clarissa,' she told him gravely. 'I don't want what we feel for one another, what we've already shared to become soured and tainted by my inability to come to terms with Clarissa's presence in your life, just as I can't allow Lucy to be exposed to Clarissa's jealousy. Don't you see, James? It isn't enough that we want one another, that we love one another. And I can't bear to stand and watch us destroying one another, because I know that's what will happen. I can't help it. I can't trust Clarissa. I don't like her. I'd never feel comfortable, or at ease. That's *my* fault, not hers.'

She paused, tears glistening in her eyes as they beseeched him to understand that this wasn't what she wanted, that what she wanted—all she wanted—was him, but how could she bear it if she gave in to that need only to discover one day that he was looking at her not with love but with resentment, with bitterness?

'No,' he agreed heavily. 'Perhaps you're right and love is not enough. I can't blame you for the way you feel about Clarissa.'

'And I can understand *your* need to protect her. Perhaps if I had a more generous nature...'

He shook his head.

'No. And you do have a generous nature.' He turned her hand over in his own and lifted it to his mouth, feathering her palm with his lips as he muttered hoarsely, '*The* most generous nature.' And then he took her in his arms, holding her tightly against him while he told her rawly, 'Oh, God,

Tania. I don't think I can bear this. To have waited so long, to have found you and then...'

'Yes,' she agreed tonelessly. 'It might almost have been better, kinder if we had not——'

'No,' he denied savagely. 'No. I can never regret having known you, having loved you... Last night... Oh, my God, Tania. Last night, I didn't use any precautions. I even hoped that you might conceive my child. I thought it would bind us closer together.'

A terrible pain gripped her. James's child... If she had conceived... But what was the point in looking for loopholes? Even if she had conceived James's child, what good would it do her? What good would it do any of them? All it would do was add to their existing burdens, to Clarissa's uncontrollable jealousy, and she would have another life to worry about, another burden of fear to carry. But James's child... Her stomach clenched and ached unbearably almost as though her womb were actually crying out for that conception.

Outside the door she could hear Lucy's voice. She pulled away from James, unable to look at him as he released her. Unable to look at anyone.

She knew that her eyes were betrayingly damp, that her whole face gave away her misery and anguish. She got up clumsily and walked over to the window, barely seeing the lovely scene outside.

Why, why had this had to happen to her? It seemed so unfair. It was so unfair.

The remainder of the day was sheer agony for her. She acquitted James of doing it deliberately; in truth she could see that he was fighting desperately hard not to respond to Lucy's obvious pleasure in his company, but to have rejected her open and eager adoration of him would have been to hurt and confuse her. Tania could see that, and yet she could not help wishing that Lucy had disliked him, had resented and rejected him. That way...that way at least only one of them would be hurt. This way they were both going to suffer.

When she tried gently to suggest leaving early, Lucy had looked so disappointed that she hadn't had the heart to insist, and so in addition to the anguish of knowing that there could be no future in loving James she had the added pain of having to acknowledge that he would have made Lucy a wonderfully caring and loving stepfather.

If only... If only what? she derided herself over the meal which Jane Williams had prepared and which she was totally unable to eat. If only Clarissa might somehow disappear in a puff of smoke. Hardly likely, and even if it were she couldn't escape the knowledge that James genuinely loved and cared about his stepsister and that anything that injured Clarissa must also injure him.

At half-past six she announced that it was time for her and Lucy to leave, and, while Lucy babbled excitedly all the way back to their own home, she remained tensely silent.

This time she had firmly seated herself in the back of the car next to Lucy, not able to trust herself not to break down and start wailing her grief, her anguish, her love, like a small child, if she gave in to the temptation of sitting next to James.

She hadn't intended to invite him in. After all they had said everything that needed to be said, everything there possibly was to be said.

He loved her, she knew that. She loved him, but as she had told him that wasn't enough. Nowhere near enough, but Lucy it seemed had other ideas. James had promised he would read her a bedtime story.

While Tania hesitated James gave her a helpless, defeated look and she knew that she had no option other than to invite him in.

She sent Lucy for her bath, made James and herself a cup of tea which they drank seated well away from one another in a strained, uncomfortable silence, and then while James read Lucy her story she busied herself in the kitchen, trying not to let herself dwell on the fact that after this evening she would only ever see him again as a stranger—as Clarissa's stepbrother, she told herself bitterly.

Quite when she started to cry she had no idea. She was numbly conscious of washing and rewashing the same mug over and over again, of tensing her body against her anguish as she heard James walk into the kitchen behind her and say jerkily, 'She's asleep. I'd better be off.'

'Yes,' she agreed brokenly.

She thought he was actually leaving until he gripped hold of her shoulders and demanded harshly, 'Is that all you can say? Is that all...?'

And then he saw her tears and through the frantically loud thudding of her heart she heard him curse and then she was in his arms, wrapped tightly

within their protective custody while he kissed her
damp face with fierce despair, telling her over and
over again that he loved her, telling her there must
be a way...

They both knew there wasn't, but that didn't stop
them from spending what was left of the evening
making frantically intensive love to one another, as
though there was a whole lifetime of loving to be
crammed into far too few short hours. As indeed
there was, Tania reflected hazily as she looked down
the length of her shadowed body to where James
lay against her, his hand against the sharp curve of
her hipbone, his mouth exploring the satin softness
of her skin.

'I love you,' he told her almost angrily. 'I love
you so much.'

'Don't,' she protested, her voice thick with tears.
'Please don't,' and then she shuddered deeply as
the pleasure of how he was loving her broke through
her grief at the parting to come and she begged him
to love her so much that she wouldn't be able to
think of anything else but this moment, so that she
would have these memories to comfort her, all the
rest of her life.

Later still, when she was loving his body as
intimately as he had done hers, she told herself that
she was surely entitled to this, that in sharing this
intimacy they were hurting no one other than
themselves, deliberately barring her mind to the
knowledge that she could already have conceived
the child who would have to grow up without a
father, and who would be hurt by this selfish,

reckless, dangerous but so wholly necessary intimacy they were sharing.

It was just gone midnight when the telephone beside her bed rang. She reached for the receiver automatically, tensing at the unexpected sound of Nicholas's voice on the other end of the line.

'Tania, it's Nicholas,' he told her. 'I've just rung Dove Court. Is James still there with you? Only we've got a bit of an emergency down here at the clinic. Clarissa isn't responding at all well to her medication. She keeps asking for James and I...'

Silently she handed the receiver to James, her eyes dark and haunted. Already it had started. Already Clarissa was coming between them, invading their most private and precious moments. Already...

Silently she slid out of her bed and found her dressing-gown, trying not to listen to James's terse voice.

He hung up after a few seconds and apologised in a tight voice, 'I'm sorry, but I'm going to have to leave.'

She had known it already, of course. Had thought she was prepared for it. Had already told herself she knew he would have to go, but she was not prepared for the pain of losing him so quickly, so abruptly, now while her body was still full of the sensation of his within it, now while she was still warm from their shared bed, while the scent of him still clung to her skin. Now when she wanted nothing more than to go to sleep in his arms, to...

But he was waiting for her to speak, to...to what? Give him permission to leave...? He didn't *need* her permission. To make it easy for him to go. She swallowed the savage, bitter words that clamoured for utterance inside her and said, as calmly as she could, 'Yes, yes. Of course.'

He was coming towards her as he dressed. Automatically she wrapped her arms around her body, rejecting him, moving back from him. She saw him hesitate, grief and pain darkening his eyes. Across the few feet of space that separated them they looked at one another and then Tania turned her back on him and said huskily, 'I'd better go in and check up on Lucy. You know the way out.'

This time she waited until she was sure he was gone. She wasn't being a coward. She was simply doing what was best for both of them. She could not have borne to watch him go, to know that it was over between them.

Over... It had barely started... She grieved for their love as she might have done for a lost early pregnancy, grieving for its right to life, to the denial of that right, as well as grieving for the life itself that would never be.

CHAPTER TEN

QUITE how she got through the following weeks, Tania really had no idea. She saw nothing of James, and heard on the grapevine that Clarissa had been flown to see a specialist in America who ran a clinic that had a spectacular record of success with her particular type of problem.

But cured or not, it made no difference. Clarissa would never really accept any other woman in James's life, and most of all not her. For as long as she was involved with James, she would never feel that Lucy was truly safe, and despite all that he had said about his stepsister she had noticed that James himself had not denied this.

Her moods alternated between ones of deep and bitter despair and frenetic bouts of energy during which she refused to allow herself to even remember that she had ever known anyone named James Warren.

Inevitably her health suffered and even more inevitably others noticed. Ann in particular, who tackled her one grey October evening when she had called round on the pretext of wanting to consult her about Susie's coming birthday.

With Lucy safely asleep in bed, Tania had no alternative but to confide in her friend when Ann asked her bluntly what was wrong.

'You've given him up...because of Clarissa!'
Ann stared at her as though she couldn't understand what she was hearing. 'But that's crazy.
Clarissa is a grown woman, a woman, moreover,
with a husband and children of her own.'

'She's almost completely emotionally dependent
on James,' Tania told her flatly, pushing her hair
off her pale, too-thin face. 'But it isn't just that.
I'm not putting myself through all this simply out
of female jealousy. There's Lucy to consider. Don't
you see, Ann? I might, just might be able to put
up with Clarissa's presence in James's life if it was
only myself I had to consider, but there's Lucy as
well.'

'You think she might try to harm Lucy again?'
Ann asked her sympathetically.

'It would always be there in a corner of my mind.'

'Yes, I can understand that, but perhaps if James
were to agree to——'

'To what? Cut her out of his life? How could I
ask him to do that, Ann? I couldn't. We're adults,
not children. I can't say to him, You say you love
me, so send her away. It wouldn't be fair, and besides I couldn't live with myself if I forced that kind
of decision on him. He loves Clarissa, and, let's
face it, if he was willing to abandon her—well,
would you want to love a man who could do that,
would you trust him? I certainly couldn't.'

'No. I can see what you mean, but there must be
a way.'

Tania shook her head sadly.

'Don't you think I've searched for one, over and
over again? If Clarissa were less emotionally un-

balanced, if it were possible to talk with her… But, well, even if she recovers this time, there's always the risk of another breakdown.'

'Oh, Tania.'

'Yes, I know,' Tania agreed shakily, 'and I'm afraid there's more.'

'More?' Ann stared at her. 'What?'

'I think I'm pregnant.'

'You're what?'

Once she got over her shock, Ann demanded anxiously, 'You *have* told James about this, haven't you? I mean, he has a right to know.'

'No, I haven't told him,' Tania interrupted her. 'I haven't even got as far as having things confirmed yet.'

'But you will tell James,' Ann insisted.

Tania closed her eyes wearily.

'Perhaps. I don't know. I just feel so tired, Ann. I feel as though I want to run away and hide from everything that's happening to me.'

Already she was regretting having told her friend so much. She wondered what Ann would say if she had also told her that virtually every single night she woke up with tears on her face and James's name on her lips.

She knew quite well that if she got in touch with him and told him she was pregnant he would move heaven and earth to get her to change her mind, and sometimes in her weakest moments she was so desperately tempted. After all, she had a right to happiness too, didn't she? Her child, their child had a right to the love of both its parents. Lucy had a right to have the loving care of a stepfather who would adore and spoil her.

But with those rights went danger. She didn't want her children exposed to Clarissa's jealousies, her paranoia and yet neither could she bear to live with the knowledge that her own happiness was built on Clarissa's misery, as it would have to be if she asked James to cut himself off from his stepsister.

Two weeks later, at Ann's insistence, she made an appointment to see her doctor and had her pregnancy confirmed.

Common sense told her that as soon as Clarissa's treatment was over and they were all back in England James was bound to discover that she was carrying his child and that if she really wanted to protect them both she ought to be making plans now to sell her shop and start a new life somewhere far away.

James had rung her several times, but on each occasion she had kept the call short.

Clarissa was responding well to her treatment, he had told her and he was managing to combine his enforced stay in America with some outstanding business he had over there. She saw Nicholas briefly on a couple of occasions and knew that he was spending all his free time either with his sons or in America with Clarissa.

Sometimes she couldn't help reflecting bitterly on how very fortunate the other woman was: a devoted husband, and an equally devoted stepbrother.

It all seemed so unfair.

And then she heard that James and Clarissa would be returning home for Christmas.

It was Jane Williams who told her. She happened to bump into her in the supermarket one afternoon when she had dashed in to do some last-minute shopping. The older woman's face lit up when she saw her, although like everyone else who knew her she exclaimed in some concern over Tania's too-slender frame and her pallor. If she suspected that these had anything to do with James's absence she was far too kind to say so.

Yes, Clarissa was responding well to the innovative American treatment, she told Tania happily, and she had received a long letter from James telling her that the whole family would be coming home for Christmas.

It was only later on her way back to her car with her shopping, when she had to stop because of the mist obscuring her vision, that Tania realised she was crying.

She was still crying hours later when Ann brought Lucy back from school, and her friend took one look at her, and then told her severely, 'Tania, Clarissa isn't going to be the only one having a breakdown.'

'I know,' she agreed, blowing her nose. 'I really must pull myself together.'

'That wasn't what I meant and you know it. You must get in touch with James. Look at yourself... and it isn't just yourself you have to consider now, is it? There's Lucy and the new baby.'

'I know. I ought to be making arrangements to sell the shop and move away, but I don't seem to have the energy to do anything. Christmas is less than a month away and——'

'Move away?' Ann was plainly aghast. 'You can't do that. And why would you want to? I thought you liked it here? The business is doing well.'

'I can't stay here now. Once James comes back——'

'You have told him about the baby, haven't you?' Ann asked her suspiciously.

Tania averted her head.

James had already asked her if she was pregnant and she had lied to him, knowing that if she told him the truth nothing would stop him from insisting on marrying her.

'Tania, you must tell him.'

'Yes, yes, I know.' She swayed suddenly, feeling cold and faint, tensing herself against the wave of weakness engulfing her as she heard Ann's shocked gasp.

'Look at you,' Ann expostulated as she helped her into a chair. 'You *can't* go on like this. You're losing weight, despite the baby. You look so frail. You're killing yourself, Tania, and if you won't consider your own health then you must consider the baby's. Unless of course you're *trying* to destroy it.'

Ann's cruelty made her eyes swim with fresh tears, but it also made her realise very sharply and painfully that Ann was right. She suddenly felt desperately cold. The last thing she wanted to do was to harm James's child, the very last thing. After all, he or she was going to be all she would ever have of the man she loved.

When Ann saw the effect her words had on her, she smiled grimly at her. 'Now you are going to get your coat on and you and Lucy are coming back with me, and you're staying with me, until I'm convinced that you're taking proper care of yourself. Otherwise . . .'

'Otherwise what?' Tania challenged shakily.

'Otherwise I shall have to tell James about the baby myself,' Ann told her quietly.

Tania stared at her, her hands crossed protectively over her stomach as she whispered pleadingly, 'No, Ann, please. You wouldn't do that.'

'I wouldn't want to,' Ann corrected her, 'but you can't go on like this.'

In the end Tania was forced to give way to her friend's motherly bullying, and she and Lucy spent a week under the Fieldings' roof, occupying their newly decorated spare-room, and using the elegant new bathroom which Ann had recently installed and on which she had practised her clever painting techniques, to marvellous effect.

As Tania told her, she particularly loved the clouds Ann had painted on the ceiling.

'When I'm lying in the bath I look up at them and make believe I'm lying on some idyllic beach,' she told Ann teasingly.

She had started to regain a little of her lost weight, but her face was still too finely drawn, her eyes and mouth haunted and shadowed with sadness.

Lucy, who had mentioned James's name virtually in every sentence she spoke for weeks after the Sunday they had spent with him, now only referred to him occasionally, but with such a wistfulness that she never failed to bring tears to Tania's eyes.

It was December and she and Ann had had several forays into Chester on Christmas buying trips. Now that she was regaining a little of her strength, Tania was determined to make this Christmas a happy and special one for Lucy.

Because she was so thin, there was no chance of anyone guessing she was pregnant and she had guiltily put off doing anything about selling her shop until after the New Year. She didn't *want* to move. She liked the town and its people. She had felt settled here, at home... but how could she stay now, bringing up James's son or daughter so close to James himself? No, it wouldn't be fair to any of them. Unacknowledged at the back of her mind lay the fact that she had already decided that James must never know she was pregnant. Once he did... Once he did, he would never let her go. And heaven alone knew how very, very tempted she would be to give in to him if he were to insist on marrying her.

As the weeks went by, she missed him more and not less; ached for him more as a man, her man, her lover...and yearned for him emotionally as well as physically, yearned to be able to share with him her joy in having conceived his child, yearned for him to be there with her, to take her in his arms and kiss away all her loneliness and pain, to tell her that everything was going to be all right and that they would always be together.

Sometimes she dreamed that it had actually happened and then she woke up to discover that she was after all alone, and the tears would come again and she would spend the rest of the night in restless agonising, in weakly wishing that somehow things might be different.

Halfway through December, she insisted on moving back to her own home.

Lucy was wildly excited about Christmas. The Fieldings and Tania and Lucy were all going out to Delamere Forest the Sunday before Christmas to buy themselves a Christmas tree, and although Tania had refused Ann's generous invitation for them to join her family for Christmas lunch she had agreed to spend the afternoon with them on Boxing Day.

Lucy was excitedly praying for snow, and the temperature was certainly dropping, although the long-range forecast did not promise a white Christmas.

And then one Sunday afternoon, when Tania was baking mince pies and Lucy was busily making and writing her Christmas cards, James arrived.

Immediately he rang the bell, Tania knew who it was, but cravenly she sent Lucy downstairs to answer it rather than going herself.

When James walked into her kitchen, she was standing defensively on the other side of her small table, watching him with wary, pain-filled eyes.

She had visualised him so often in her dreams, in her most private and intimate thoughts, remembering him, aching for him, that the shock of seeing

him in the flesh and of realising that like her he
had suffered destroyed her hard-won composure.

She could feel the emotion clogging her throat,
the weakness enveloping her body.

He too had lost weight. He too had suffered and
known pain, and for a moment all she wanted to
do was to step out from behind the table and to
hold him in her arms.

As though he sensed her need, he took a step
towards her and immediately she tensed, remembering why she must not weaken.

'Don't come too close,' she warned him. 'I'm
covered in flour and it will ruin your suit. I heard
you were all coming back for Christmas. Have you
been back long? And Clarissa...is she well?'

She was chattering non-stop, trying to fill the
aching void of pain welling up inside her, trying to
stop herself from cravenly bursting into tears and
telling him that no matter what she just could not
live without him.

'We flew in on this morning's transatlantic
flight,' he told her quietly. 'Clarissa is fine. Tania...
please——'

He broke off as Lucy came into the kitchen.

'Here's your card,' she told him importantly.
'Mum said I could send you one, but I might as
well give it to you now.'

James bent down and picked her up, and to
Tania's consternation told her gruffly, 'Why not
keep it for me until Christmas Day?' And then,
looking directly at Tania, he told her quietly, 'I want
you and your mummy to come and spend Christmas
with me at my house, Lucy. Would you like that?'

'Will Rupert be there?' Lucy asked him.

James laughed.

'Yes, Rupert will be there.'

How could he do this to her? How dared he use Lucy against her like that? He knew she could not, must not accept such an invitation...

'I'm sorry,' she began stiffly, formally, 'But I'm afraid that's impossible——'

She stopped and made the mistake of looking at him. The pain, the love, the agony in his eyes twisted her heart and made her want to cry out to him that nothing else mattered other than him.

'Nothing's impossible,' he told her huskily.

At her side, Lucy was pleading with her, begging her to say yes, leaning her head against her, so that she was immediately and emotionally conscious of James's child, as yet unnoticeable, but growing there within her none the less, and even though it was the last thing she had intended to say she heard herself accepting shakily and agreeing that, yes, they would spend Christmas at Dove Court with him.

After that it seemed that she was caught up in a roller-coaster, so speedily did James insist on making all the arrangements. He would collect them on Christmas Eve and they would spend until after the New Year with him.

'It's too long,' she protested. 'Christmas Day... Boxing Day...'

'Too long?'

The smile he gave her was brief and bitter and inside her a small voice demanded rebelliously that she give in, that she allow herself this last small space of time with him.

When she told Ann, apologising that they would not after all be seeing them on Boxing Day, her friend was not in the least offended.

'I'm delighted you've come to your senses at last,' she told Tania frankly, totally misunderstanding the situation. 'Have you told him about the baby yet?'

'Er—no...'

'Saving it for Christmas Day?' Ann asked her with a knowing smile. 'A very special present for him.'

Tania said nothing. She had no intention of telling James about their child. She had been weak enough as it was in giving in to his invitation to spend Christmas with him.

Since Christmas Eve fell on a Sunday, there was no necessity to open the shop but even so Tania was startled to find James had arrived while she and Lucy were still having their breakfast.

Fortunately they were already virtually packed, right down to the brightly wrapped present which Lucy had insisted on choosing for James all by herself. Privately Tania wasn't sure that he would totally appreciate a china replica of Rupert, but she hadn't had the heart to say so to Lucy.

She herself had merely bought him a tie, a plain silk one, anonymous in the extreme and in no way to be compared with the gift she had already given him, nor the one she herself had received from him in turn.

Her child...*their* child... She touched her stomach lightly and then tensed as James followed the movement and asked her tersely, 'Are you all right?'

'Yes, of course,' she told him brittly. 'Why shouldn't I be?'

He said nothing, but she could see his eyes measuring the loss of weight.

'You're a little earlier than I expected,' she told him.

'That's because I need Lucy's help with the tree,' he told her, smiling at Lucy's ecstatically delighted smile.

'Is it a very big tree?' she asked him later, as they left the flat. Tania couldn't help noticing the trusting, natural way Lucy slipped her hand into James's as they walked out into the street.

'Fairly big,' James told her.

'Well, I might not be able to reach to the top,' Lucy told him anxiously. 'Will——?'

'Don't worry. I'll do the high bits,' James reassured her.

They had had a sharp frost overnight and as the Jaguar turned in between Dove Court's pretty gate houses the lawns were still white and crisp with their riming of frost, so that Lucy caught her breath in delight, and Tania felt her heart ache with melancholic grief.

She must make this holiday a happy one, she told herself as James drove up the drive. She must store up from it only good memories, only happy thoughts, not just for Lucy's sake but for the sake of the child in her womb as well. Perhaps it was fanciful of her to believe that somehow that child could sense her mood, could be affected by her misery, and could also surely sense her happiness as well, and might somehow come to know of the great love she had shared with its father if only she could put aside her grief and pain and allow herself to believe that this wretchedly brief span of time they would have together could last for ever.

She forced herself to concentrate on this as James stopped the car and came to help her out.

Just the mere touch of his hand on her arm was enough to make her acutely aware of how much she loved him. She had already noticed that he was careful not to touch her, not to torment her or himself by reminding both of what they could not have.

James opened the front door and shepherded them inside, and then Tania froze in shock as she saw Clarissa there.

She looked accusingly and bitterly at James. Somehow she had never expected this. She had not even asked him about Clarissa because she had assumed that he would never risk having them both in the same house. And yet she realised she ought to have asked him, ought to have at least made some enquiries as to where Clarissa would be spending Christmas.

James returned her look, aware of her anger and despair. He took a step towards her and she stepped back from him, feeling her body grow tense with anguish.

She was just about to call out to Lucy, to insist that James took them home immediately when she saw that Clarissa was approaching her daughter.

Immediately she started forwards, but James gripped her arm stopping her.

While she glared at him in outrage, she heard Clarissa saying easily, 'Hello, Lucy. I don't know if you remember me?'

'Yes. Rupert lives with you, doesn't he,' Lucy responded a little shyly.

Tania, frozen within James's silent custody, stared at them, her heart pounding with anger and fear. How dared James do this to her . . . and why? What was the purpose of this dangerous charade?

'Yes, he does,' Clarissa agreed. She turned to Tania.

'Tania, it's lovely to see you,' she greeted her warmly. 'I'm looking forward to us all getting together tomorrow, and the boys are both longing to meet Lucy.'

Tania stared at her, unable to believe her ears, unable to believe her eyes as she focused on this new, unbelievably relaxed woman who had Clarissa's face and voice, and yet who seemed to be a completely different woman from the one Tania remembered.

Before Tania could say anything, the sitting-room door opened and Clarissa's two sons came out, accompanied by Nicholas and Rupert. Whilst Lucy bent down to fuss the dog who obviously remembered her, Clarissa was saying to her husband, 'Nicky, darling, why don't you take Lucy and the boys for a walk? We could do with some more holly and I think there's some with berries on the tree down by the lake.' She came towards Tania and took hold of her free arm. 'I'll show you up to your room, Tania.'

Like a dream walker, Tania went with her, pausing on the stairs to give James a confused, angry look.

As they walked upstairs together, Clarissa kept up a gentle, meaningless flow of chatter in a soft, reassuring voice that Tania realised half hysterically was meant to soothe her. What was happening here? Why hadn't James warned her?

'James has put you in this room,' Clarissa told her, opening one of the doors and going inside so that Tania had no option but to follow her.

'This was originally the master bedroom,' she heard Clarissa telling her. 'Of course I expect you'll want to redecorate it. I know my mother did when she married James's father. It's a lovely house, isn't it, although it does need a woman's touch? When we lived here mother always kept every room filled with flowers. She enjoyed living here so much. We both did. I think after the loneliness and poverty of the years without my father, to come and live here——'

She broke off when Tania stared at her and then demanded huskily, 'What do you mean, I'll want to redecorate it?'

Clarissa turned round and looked directly at her.

'I know about you and James, Tania,' she told her quietly. 'I can't deny that at first I was... I felt deserted, bereft... I was very, very angry, hysterical really, and very, very jealous, but Dr Martin—he's my therapist at the clinic in California... Well, he's helped me to understand that my dependence on James all springs from my feelings towards my father; the great sense of loss and guilt I felt when he left my mother. He's helped me to understand that there were emotions locked up inside me, left over from that time, which were poisoning my whole life and not just mine. I won't bore you with all the details of my therapy, of my growing up, if you like. It wasn't always a painless or an easy process, but I feel I have learned from it. I may not ever be the kind of woman who never feels an atom of jealousy. I'll probably always be inclined to be possessive of those closest to me, but at least now I know that trait within myself and I've learned how to deal with it.

'Dr Martin helped me to understand how much my jealousy was damaging not just me but everyone around me, how I was destroying them along with myself.

'I was so pleased with myself because I was responding well to the treatment. I couldn't understand why James was so remote, so...so very obviously unhappy, and then he told me about you. I can't deny that at first I *was* bitterly resentful. I won't tell you about the scenes I staged, about the mean, cruel things I said, not just about you but about James as well. I even told him that he had to choose between us.' Her voice almost broke but she continued firmly, 'A stupid thing to do, and it served me right when he told me that he would always, always choose you. He then went on to tell me that you had refused to ask him to make such a choice; that you were wise enough, generous enough, loving enough to know that I would always

have a special place in his heart, in his life. Then
he told me that he couldn't live without you. That
you were as necessary to him as air itself.

'I had to work very hard to accept that, Tania.
To make myself not merely accept outwardly, but
to accept inwardly as well that another woman
meant more to James than me, that you would
always have first place in his heart, whether you
were there with him in person or not.

'Yes, it was very, very hard for me to accept that.
It was Nick who helped me, who told me that I was
destroying James, that I was hurting one of the
people I professed to love. What would happen
when the boys grew up, he asked? Would I prevent
them from finding happiness just as I was pre-
venting James? Would I turn them away from me,
make them hate and resent me?

'I accused him of not loving me. He told me that
he had always loved me, that he had married me
even though he had feared that I loved someone
else. He even told me...' she took a deep breath
'...he even told me that at times he had doubted
that Alec was his child, but that he loved him
anyway because he was mine.

'I was so shocked. I had had no idea. Of course
Alec is his, and I love him too... I always have
done... My affair with...with someone else had
meant nothing. I just let Nick think it did because
I was so unsure of him.

'Two weeks ago, I walked into James's room and
I found him sitting there with his head in his hands,
and tears pouring down his face. I was so shocked.
He'd always seemed so strong, so inviolate. I'd

never seen him like that before, never thought of him as being vulnerable. I asked him what was wrong. He told me that you were refusing to speak to him. He told me that you'd refused to marry him. That you felt you couldn't make a commitment to him because of me. Is that true, Tania?'

Tania looked at her, and then moistened her lips. She had no idea how to deal with this new Clarissa, or what to say to her.

When she remained silent, Clarissa said unsteadily. 'Very well, I'll ask you another question. Do you love James?'

The look on her face gave her away before Tania spoke.

'That's all that matters, really, isn't it?' Clarissa told her softly. 'You love him and he loves you. Your place is with James just as mine is with my husband. I know now that I will always have a place in James's heart, that in marrying he won't be excluding me from his life...

'I want you to know, Tania, that James's happiness is far more important to me than my own fear and jealousy. James needs you far more than he needs me, and I'm strong enough now to let him go, to live my own life with my own husband and children and to let James live his with you...and just to prove it...' She turned her back to Tania and walked over to the window, staring out of it for several seconds before saying huskily, 'Just to prove it, Nick and I have decided to start a new life together in California. We both like it out there. Dr Martin believes it's a good step for me to take. That putting some physical distance between myself and James is all a good part of my recovery. I don't say I'm not going to miss him, that there won't be times when I just can't stop myself from picking up the phone and speaking to him, but I do promise you that you need never fear that either you, or any child of yours, either Lucy or any child you might have with James, will ever suffer in any way through me.

'When I came to my senses and realised what I'd done to Lucy...' She gave a deep shudder. 'I think I'd kill anyone who tried to harm either of my own two.' Her voice dropped. 'I wanted to end my own life when I realised what I had done. Paying someone to break your window was one thing, but that... I won't ask you to forgive me. How could you? It's more than I deserve that you were prepared to sacrifice your own happiness rather than to ask James to cut me out of his life.'

'He loves you,' Tania told her shakily, finding her voice at last. 'How could I ask him?'

'And yet I would so easily and so thoughtlessly have asked...no, demanded that he give *you* up,' Clarissa said sadly. 'When I think of the harm I've done, the unhappiness I've caused. Not just to you and James, but to Nick and the boys as well. I intend to make it up to them, to show them that I do love them and that I am capable of loving them less selfishly. I'm so lucky...I could so easily have lost Nick.'

'Not to me,' Tania assured her gravely.

Clarissa smiled at her.

'No, not to you, but to someone far less scrupulous than you and I would have deserved it. I was a bitch to him at times.'

'You were ill,' Tania told her.

'My illness was self-induced. Oh, I don't have any pity for myself,' she told her firmly. 'Why should I? I reserve my pity for my victims, for all those I've hurt through my selfishness. You will marry James, won't you?'

Tania hesitated. It was almost too much for her to take in. Almost like something unreal...like one of her impossible, tormenting dreams.

'I...'

'I promise you, you need fear nothing from me,' Clarissa reiterated. 'Neither you, nor Lucy, nor the new baby you're carrying.'

Tania stared at her, her face going white, her hands crossed protectively against her stomach. 'How did you...? No one...'

'A man might be deceived into thinking that it's a broken heart that's responsible for so much weight loss and pallor; a woman knows better, especially when both her own pregnancies began with twelve weeks of unremitting morning sickness,' Clarissa told her grimly.

Suddenly Tania discovered that she was crying. Huge gulping sobs that tore at her throat and chest, and then she was in Clarissa's arms and Clarissa was soothing her, reassuring her, and suddenly, instinctively somehow she knew that it was true and that she need have nothing to fear for her family from James's stepsister.

'I hope James can't hear you crying,' Clarissa scolded her gently. 'He must be distraught by now, wondering what on earth's going on. He would have told you everything himself, but I wanted to tell you myself. I thought you might believe me.'

'I do,' Tania told her shakily, blowing her nose. 'And don't think I don't understand how hard it must have been for you. James has told me about...about your childhood and your father.'

'Yes. Another reason why I went so crazy when I thought I was losing Nick to you. I've always sworn I would never let a child of mine suffer what I went through, and yet I was the one who was endangering our marriage, who was putting them at risk. Lucy...does she...?'

'No after-effects at all,' Tania assured her.

'Thank God for that.' She pressed Tania's hand and told her softly, 'Why don't you go and find James and put him out of his misery? I'll go out and collect the others. Would it be all right if Lucy comes back with us tonight or...?'

This was the true test. Tania looked at her and wondered if she had the strength to make the act of faith it demanded...if she could bring herself to entrust her precious Lucy to this woman who had so dangerously wanted to harm her.

'No...of course you couldn't——' Clarissa began, turning away from her.

Tania stopped her and said shakily, 'Do you think Lucy would ever forgive me if I denied her the opportunity to spend a whole night with her beloved Rupert?'

And suddenly they both were laughing and crying at the same time, hugging one another, and Tania knew without question that one day she and this woman would share a very special closeness, that this bonding just beginning between them would enrich them both all through their lives.

Tania and James had Christmas Eve all to themselves. They spent it curled up in front of the sitting-room fire making plans.

James wanted an early wedding, as early as possible so that the ceremony could take place before Clarissa and Nicholas flew back to California in the New Year.

'We're going to be so happy together,' he promised her. 'We're going to make up for every single moment of heartache and misery we've both known.'

'Starting when?' Tania teased him as she stroked her fingertips lovingly along the line of his jaw, her lips pouting provocatively only inches from his own.

She had never known what it was like to play like this, to feel free and young like this, to tease like this, and be punished for it, if indeed it was punishment when James took hold of her and kissed her ruthlessly into silence as he muttered against her lips, 'Starting right now!'

It was midnight before she realised that she still hadn't told him about their child. They had just made love lying together in front of the fire, and as she nestled rosy and content in his arms she reached up and whispered to him, 'I've got a very special Christmas present for you if you'd like it.'

He opened his eyes and protested lazily, 'What, again? You're insatiable, do you know that?'

Tania protested and then told him haughtily, 'That *wasn't* what I meant at all. We're going to have a baby.'

She had his attention now; he rolled over and stared down at her and asked with bewildered male awe, 'Are we? How can you tell so soon?'

So soon? Tania stared at him and then burst out laughing.

'James! Not because of now. I'm *already* pregnant. The baby's due in five and a half months.'

For a moment he was completely still and then he said unsteadily, 'Do you mean to tell me that all this time ... and you weren't going to say a word?'

'I wanted to,' she assured him shakily. 'I wanted to more than you'll ever know ... but how could I? I knew if I did you'd insist on marrying me and then I'd have to live with the knowledge that because of me you'd have had to cut yourself off from Clarissa.'

'So you knew I'd have done that for you.'

'Yes,' she told him, 'but I couldn't have lived with it on my conscience.'

'I ought to be furious with you. You realise that ... but, somehow ... I feel far too happy.'

'Mm, me too.' She kissed him lingeringly and then whispered provocatively, 'Now it's your turn to give me my present.'

He looked at her, a long lazy male look that swept the soft curves of her body where she lay highlighted by the firelight and then he said softly to her, 'Well, now, my love, what is it exactly you have in mind?'

When she told him, he kissed her again and said lovingly, 'I was right the first time. You are insatiable.'

On Christmas morning after the initial excitement of opening presents was over and before they all sat down to lunch which Tania and Clarissa had prepared between them, James uncorked a chilled bottle of champagne, ceremoniously filled their glasses and announced with a grin, 'Tania and I have something to tell you——'

'Two somethings actually,' Tania interrupted him, and then added with a smile, 'And one request.'

After they had announced their plans to marry and the arrival of the baby, Nicholas asked them, 'And what was the request?'

'Oh, that.' Tania smiled across at Clarissa and said quietly, 'Nothing much. Just that we'd like you and Clarissa to be godparents.'

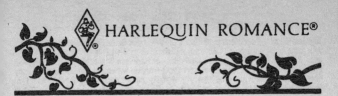

HARLEQUIN ROMANCE®

**Harlequin Romance
knows love can be dangerous!**

Don't miss
TO LOVE AND PROTECT (#3223)
by Kate Denton,
the October title in

THE BRIDAL COLLECTION

THE GROOM'S life was in peril.
THE BRIDE was hired to help him.
BUT THEIR WEDDING was *more* than
a business arrangement!

Available this month in
The Bridal Collection
JACK OF HEARTS (#3218)
by Heather Allison
Wherever Harlequin books are sold.

OFFICIAL RULES • MILLION DOLLAR WISHBOOK SWEEPSTAKES
NO PURCHASE OR OBLIGATION NECESSARY TO ENTER

To enter, follow the directions published. If the Wishbook Game Card is missing, hand-print your name and address on a 3″ ×5″ card and mail to either: Harlequin Wishbook, 3010 Walden Ave., P.O. Box 1867, Buffalo, NY 14269-1867, or Harlequin Wishbook, P.O. Box 609, Fort Erie, Ontario L2A 5X3, and upon receipt of your entry we will assign you Sweepstakes numbers (Limit: one entry per envelope). For eligibility, entries must be received no later than March 31, 1994 and be sent via 1st-class mail. No liability is assumed for printing errors or lost, late or misdirected entries.

To determine winners, the Sweepstakes numbers on submitted entries will be compared against a list of randomly, pre-selected prizewinning numbers. In the event all prizes are not claimed via the return of prizewinning numbers, random drawings will be held from among all other entries received to award unclaimed prizes.

Prizewinners will be determined no later than May 30, 1994. Selection of winning numbers and random drawings are under the supervision of D.L. Blair, Inc., an independent judging organization whose decisions are final. One prize to a family or organization. No substitution will be made for any prize, except as offered. Taxes and duties on all prizes are the sole responsibility of winners. Winners will be notified by mail. Chances of winning are determined by the number of entries distributed and received.

Sweepstakes open to persons 18 years of age or older, except employees and immediate family members of Torstar Corporation, D.L. Blair, Inc., their affiliates, subsidiaries and all other agencies, entities and persons connected with the use, marketing or conduct of this Sweepstakes. All applicable laws and regulations apply. Sweepstakes offer void wherever prohibited by law. Any litigation within the province of Quebec respecting the conduct and awarding of a prize in this Sweepstakes must be submitted to the Régies des Loteries et Courses du Quebec. In order to win a prize, residents of Canada will be required to correctly answer a time-limited arithmetical skill-testing question. Values of all prizes are in U.S. currency.

Winners of major prizes will be obligated to sign and return an affidavit of eligibility and release of liability within 30 days of notification. In the event of non-compliance within this time period, prize may be awarded to an alternate winner. Any prize or prize notification returned as undeliverable will result in the awarding of the prize to an alternate winner. By acceptance of their prize, winners consent to use of their names, photographs or other likenesses for purposes of advertising, trade and promotion on behalf of Torstar Corporation without further compensation, unless prohibited by law.

This Sweepstakes is presented by Torstar Corporation, its subsidiaries and affiliates in conjunction with book, merchandise and/or product offerings. Prizes are as follows: Grand Prize—$1,000,000 (payable at $33,333.33 a year for 30 years). First through Sixth Prizes may be presented in different creative executions, each with the following approximate values: First Prize—$35,000; Second Prize—$10,000; 2 Third Prizes—$5,000 each; 5 Fourth Prizes—$1,000 each; 10 Fifth Prizes—$250 each; 1,000 Sixth Prizes—$100 each. Prizewinners will have the opportunity of selecting any prize offered for that level. A travel-prize option if offered and selected by winner, must be completed within 12 months of selection and is subject to hotel and flight accommodations availability. Torstar Corporation may present this Sweepstakes utilizing names other than Million Dollar Sweepstakes. For a current list of all prize options offered within prize levels and all names the Sweepstakes may utilize, send a self-addressed stamped envelope (WA residents need not affix return postage) to: Million Dollar Sweepstakes Prize Options/Names, P.O. Box 4710, Blair, NE 68009.

For a list of prizewinners (available after July 31, 1994) send a separate, stamped self-addressed envelope to: Million Dollar Sweepstakes Winners, P.O. Box 4728, Blair NE 68009.

The Extra Bonus Prize will be awarded in a random drawing to be conducted no later than 5/30/94 from among all entries received. To qualify, entries must be received by 3/31/94 and comply with published directions. No purchase necessary. For complete rules, send a self-addressed, stamped envelope (WA residents need not affix return postage) to: Extra Bonus Prize Rules, P.O. Box 4600, Blair, NE 68009.

SW9-92